A
wi

The Executioner threw himself flat as a wild, ragged spray of rounds slapped out in his direction. He hit the pavement hard and grunted.

Bolan thrust his arm out straight and rolled over onto his side as he tried to target the charging man. Still firing, the man shuffled toward the nominal protection of a dented car. He went to one knee behind the bumper of the dark blue vehicle and brought his weapon to his shoulder.

Bolan didn't hesitate. He rolled onto his stomach and took his Glock in both hands. His first shot hit wide of the gas hatch. His second punctured it. A jet of gasoline shot out in an arc and splashed the ground.

Bolan squeezed his trigger twice and put two more bullets through the bleeding gas tank. The second bullet ignited the flammable gasses trapped inside. A ball of flame erupted and was followed hard by a wave of concussive force. It was like hell on earth.

MACK BOLAN®
The Executioner

- #266 Ultimate Price
- #267 Invisible Invader
- #268 Shattered Trust
- #269 Shifting Shadows
- #270 Judgment Day
- #271 Cyberhunt
- #272 Stealth Striker
- #273 UForce
- #274 Rogue Target
- #275 Crossed Borders
- #276 Leviathan
- #277 Dirty Mission
- #278 Triple Reverse
- #279 Fire Wind
- #280 Fear Rally
- #281 Blood Stone
- #282 Jungle Conflict
- #283 Ring of Retaliation
- #284 Devil's Army
- #285 Final Strike
- #286 Armageddon Exit
- #287 Rogue Warrior
- #288 Arctic Blast
- #289 Vendetta Force
- #290 Pursued
- #291 Blood Trade
- #292 Savage Game
- #293 Death Merchants
- #294 Scorpion Rising
- #295 Hostile Alliance
- #296 Nuclear Game
- #297 Deadly Pursuit
- #298 Final Play
- #299 Dangerous Encounter
- #300 Warrior's Requiem
- #301 Blast Radius
- #302 Shadow Search
- #303 Sea of Terror
- #304 Soviet Specter
- #305 Point Position
- #306 Mercy Mission
- #307 Hard Pursuit
- #308 Into the Fire
- #309 Flames of Fury
- #310 Killing Heat
- #311 Night of the Knives
- #312 Death Gamble
- #313 Lockdown
- #314 Lethal Payload
- #315 Agent of Peril
- #316 Poison Justice
- #317 Hour of Judgment
- #318 Code of Resistance
- #319 Entry Point
- #320 Exit Code
- #321 Suicide Highway
- #322 Time Bomb
- #323 Soft Target
- #324 Terminal Zone
- #325 Edge of Hell
- #326 Blood Tide
- #327 Serpent's Lair
- #328 Triangle of Terror
- #329 Hostile Crossing
- #330 Dual Action
- #331 Assault Force
- #332 Slaughter House
- #333 Aftershock
- #334 Jungle Justice
- #335 Blood Vector
- #336 Homeland Terror
- #337 Tropic Blast
- #338 Nuclear Reaction
- #339 Deadly Contact
- #340 Splinter Cell
- #341 Rebel Force

The Executioner
Don Pendleton's
REBEL FORCE

A GOLD EAGLE BOOK FROM
W✪RLDWIDE

TORONTO • NEW YORK • LONDON
AMSTERDAM • PARIS • SYDNEY • HAMBURG
STOCKHOLM • ATHENS • TOKYO • MILAN
MADRID • WARSAW • BUDAPEST • AUCKLAND

If you purchased this book without a cover you should be aware that this book is stolen property. It was reported as "unsold and destroyed" to the publisher, and neither the author nor the publisher has received any payment for this "stripped book."

First edition April 2007
ISBN-13: 978-0-373-64341-7
ISBN-10: 0-373-64341-1

Special thanks and acknowledgment to
Nathan Meyer for his contribution to this work.

REBEL FORCE

Copyright © 2007 by Worldwide Library.

All rights reserved. Except for use in any review, the reproduction or utilization of this work in whole or in part in any form by any electronic, mechanical or other means, now known or hereafter invented, including xerography, photocopying and recording, or in any information storage or retrieval system, is forbidden without the written permission of the publisher, Worldwide Library, 225 Duncan Mill Road, Don Mills, Ontario, Canada M3B 3K9.

All characters in this book have no existence outside the imagination of the author and have no relation whatsoever to anyone bearing the same name or names. They are not even distantly inspired by any individual known or unknown to the author, and all incidents are pure invention.

® and TM are trademarks of the publisher. Trademarks indicated with ® are registered in the United States Patent and Trademark Office, the Canadian Trade Marks Office and in other countries.

Printed in U.S.A.

Cowards falter, but danger is often overcome by those who nobly dare.
—Elizabeth I, 1533–1603

People acting out of cowardice make mistakes. When they do, I will be ready to take action.
—Mack Bolan

THE
MACK BOLAN

LEGEND

Nothing less than a war could have fashioned the destiny of the man called Mack Bolan. Bolan earned the Executioner title in the jungle hell of Vietnam.

But this soldier also wore another name—Sergeant Mercy. He was so tagged because of the compassion he showed to wounded comrades-in-arms and Vietnamese civilians.

Mack Bolan's second tour of duty ended prematurely when he was given emergency leave to return home and bury his family, victims of the Mob. Then he declared a one-man war against the Mafia.

He confronted the Families head-on from coast to coast, and soon a hope of victory began to appear. But Bolan had broken society's every rule. That same society started gunning for this elusive warrior—to no avail.

So Bolan was offered amnesty to work within the system against terrorism. This time, as an employee of Uncle Sam, Bolan became Colonel John Phoenix. With a command center at Stony Man Farm in Virginia, he and his new allies—Able Team and Phoenix Force—waged relentless war on a new adversary: the KGB.

But when his one true love, April Rose, died at the hands of the Soviet terror machine, Bolan severed all ties with Establishment authority.

Now, after a lengthy lone-wolf struggle and much soul-searching, the Executioner has agreed to enter an "arm's-length" alliance with his government once more, reserving the right to pursue personal missions in his Everlasting War.

The factory sat on the banks of the Sunzha River. As silent as a mausoleum, the building was surrounded by warehouses and industrial structures all bombed to rubble in the wake of the second Chechen war. An expensive black Mercedes sat abandoned in the half-acre parking lot. The sky was starless under close cloud cover. Rain fell, dirty gray from the sky.

Mack Bolan drew his mouth into a tight line. He scanned the building and the area around it through his night-vision goggles. He searched for telltale smeary silhouettes in the monochromatic green of the high-tech device but saw nothing. Even the engine block on the Mercedes was cool. The sounds of traffic came to him from other areas of the city, muted across the distance. Close by, his ears detected only the whisper of cold wind skipping across the polluted river.

Bolan scrutinized the building, determining his approach. To the rear of the building loading docks with big roll-up bay doors sat shut and locked. The front of the building was made up of wide glass windows, and revolving doors that led into the company front offices. If Bolan approached from that direction, he'd have his back to the access road and an impossibly wide front to cover.

On the side of the building closest to him a maintenance door was set at the top of a short flight of concrete steps. Off in the distance, Bolan heard the rotors of a helicopter cruising low over the city. The Executioner's finely honed battle instincts whispered to him. Danger lay on every side.

The Mercedes, parked in the open, with no attempt at concealment or subterfuge in a city under martial law, was an enigma. Bolan wanted to be the wild card, not have some high-end vehicle fill that role. Sitting there, sleek and black and silent, it announced a human presence in a location supposedly long abandoned.

Bolan again scanned the area.

Grozny had been locked down under the threat of terrorist action by Chechen separatists. Police units patrolled in armored personnel carriers and army checkpoints secured every major road and highway leading into the city. Russia's federal army worked hard at a three-point mission. Keep the oil flowing, keep the rebel insurgency suppressed and minimize troop casualties. Those protocols had resulted in an occupying force prone to using their weapons more than restraint.

Bolan knew he had taken a grave risk by going armed into the sovereign territory of an allied nation dealing with the threat of a violent insurrection. It was an insurrection with increasingly solidified ties to the worldwide jihadist movement. Moving incognito, Bolan had flown into Grozny using Associated Press credentials as Matt Cooper, freelance reporter.

Hal Brognola from Justice had secured the location of a cache drop used by CIA paramilitary teams during the Chechen wars. Slipping free from his state-sponsored monitors, Bolan had managed to get to the drop and secure money, equipment and a Kevlar armor vest, as well as personal weapons.

Bolan moved forward, scrambling out of the empty drainage ditch that ran parallel to the building. He approached a chain-link fence and dropped down, removing wire cutters from his combat harness. Using deft, practiced movements, Bolan snipped an opening and bent back one edge.

Bolan slid through headfirst and popped up on the other side. Traveling in a wide crescent, designed to take him as far as possible from the Mercedes, Bolan approached the maintenance entrance. He scanned the triple row of windows set above the building's ground floor for any sign of movement. As he neared the building, Bolan pulled a Glock 17 from his shoulder rig.

Bolan crept up the short flight of stairs leading to the door, clicking the selector switch on his pistol off safety as he moved. Reaching the door, Bolan pulled a lock pick gun from a cargo pocket and slid it expertly home. He pulled the trigger on the locksmith device and heard the bolt securing the door snap back. Replacing the lock pick gun, Bolan put a hand on the door handle, holding his 9 mm pistol up and ready.

He thought about the intelligence intercept that had come through at the last moment. Because of strained relations with the Russian government over the Iraq war and the status of Iran's nuclear program, the Oval Office had decided to keep America's ally out of the loop. Enzik Garabend, an Armenian middleman responsible for financial networks and communications between disparate terror cells, was on his way to the Chechen capital. A meet had been planned with Kamir Abdhula Zanibar, head of a violent, Whabbism influenced, splinter militia of the main Chechen separatist movement.

In order to make use of the real-time information, Brognola had been forced to rush Bolan into place. Garabend was known never to be without his laptop. Encrypted inside of its software was believed to be a blueprint to the worldwide financial networks of the global jihad, linking Abu Sayef in Southeast Asia, with Islamic Jihad and al Qaeda in the Middle East, all the way to EU splinter groups and Chechen field commanders. It was a brass ring worth killing for.

Before he moved he took a final scan of his surroundings. The industrial wasteland was eerily still. Taking a breath, the Executioner turned the handle and pulled the door open. He stepped through the black mouth of the open door and into the darkened interior of the building. He shuffled smoothly to one side, sank into a tight crouch, pistol up, and let the door swing shut behind him.

Bolan quickly took in the hall in both directions. It was empty. Rising, he began moving down the corridor toward the rear of the building.

The building was oppressively still and quiet around him. The perimeter hallway ran the length of the structure, with doors leading to the building's interior spaced at intervals along the inside wall. At the far end Bolan could make out the heavy steel of a fire door that would open to stairs.

The intelligence on the building layout had been spotty. The factory had served many functions over the years and had played little part in the Chechen insurrection or in Russian oil concerns. All Bolan knew was that Garabend, with his bodyguards, would be in an office suite on the second floor for seven hours before departing Grozny for Damascus.

Bolan entered the stairwell. He craned his neck, looking upward. Nothing moved on the stairs or crouched in the gloomy landings. He tracked his scanning vision with the poised muzzle of the Glock 17. The hair on the back of Bolan's neck stood raised like the hackles of a dog.

The stale smell of dust and disuse was hanging heavy in the air. Faintly beneath that was the slight odor of machine oil coming up from the factory floor. Bolan's straining ears detected nothing. He placed the reinforced soles of his boots carefully on the first metal rung of the building's skeletal framed staircase and began to climb.

He edged around the curve of the stair. The raised grip of the pistol's butt snuggled tightly into his palms. He kept his Weaver stance tight, keyed-up to react to the slightest motion. Garabend was an established veteran of life as a hunted man. Security so apparently lax was unexplainable in such a man.

Reaching the second-floor landing, Bolan snuggled up tight against the fire door. He pressed his back against the wall beside the door handle. The seal of the landing door was too tight for him to use a fiber optics surveillance cable borescope. The heavy steel door effectively muted any potential sound coming from the second-floor hallway.

Gritting his teeth, Bolan pulled the door open and darted his head around the edge. He was met with silence and darkness. The hallway ran for several yards, office doors on one side, dark windows facing the parking lot on the other. The hall turned in a L-break at the far end toward the front of the building.

Bolan moved down the center of the hallway, ready to drop prone or respond with deadly fire at the slightest threat. He moved as silently as his considerable skills allowed, but to his own adrenaline-enhanced hearing, his footfalls echoed loudly. Reaching the bend in the hallway, Bolan took a rapid look around the corner. Along this stretch, doorways marked both sides of the hall at intermittent lengths.

Halfway down he picked out a crumpled form. From the green smear under the still shape, Bolan could tell the figure had lost a lot of blood, and recently, as the signature still held a good amount of heat. Instinctively Bolan snapped his line of sight up, scanning the corridor for any sign of movement. Seeing none, Bolan slid around the corner and into the passage.

The heat register meant the downed figure was either still alive, or had been struck down just minutes before. Keeping low, Bolan moved forward. His nostrils flared under the saddle of the night-vision goggles. The reek of cordite was heavy on the stale air of the abandoned factory.

Going up to the body, Bolan looked it over quickly. The figure remained still. Reaching his free hand out, Bolan felt for a pulse on the figure's neck, found none. He peered down, straining to make out facial features in the ambivalent light of the NVGs. The figure was male. A thick beard fell across a broad swell of chest. He was dressed in a Russian army pattern camouflage parka. There was a folding stock, paratrooper model AKS-74 under the man's body.

Bolan touched the barrel. The metal was cool. The weapon had not been fired. Scanning the hallway, Bolan used his fingers to probe the corpse, trying to ascertain the source of his injuries. The face was intact, the torso clear of wounds. Frowning, Bolan felt the back of the man's head.

His fingers came away wet.

The location on the back of the head where the spinal cord merged with the back of skull was the medulla oblongata, Latin for "stem of the rose." Bolan knew it was the collective location for all of the nerves of the central nervous system. The hypothalamus hung there like a grape cluster, regulating breath and the beating of the heart. In the special operations community, a shot to the medulla oblongata was known as "popping the grape" and was a preferred method of neutralizing subjects from behind.

This hadn't been a sloppy assassination. The dead man—Chechen, Bolan guessed, given the beard and Russian army jacket—had been coolly dispatched from up close and personal by someone with the nerves of a professional killer.

Bolan rose and stepped over the corpse. The man had been killed directly in front of a door on the outer side of the hallway. His intelligence information hadn't been specific as to where on the second floor Garabend was supposed to be having his meeting.

"This mission is going to be very ad hoc, Striker," Brognola had warned.

Bolan knew ad hoc was government speak for "half-assed."

Bolan also knew that, in his War Everlasting, "half-assed" got you killed. But he felt, just as Brognola did, that the information on Garabend's laptop was worth the risk. Worth his life even, if every drop of his blood was counted against the blood of innocents. Innocents Bolan had sworn his life to defend and avenge.

Bolan put his hand on the office door.

It swung open easily under his touch.

The Executioner glided into the room, pistol tracking ahead of him. The room was a reception area leading, presumably, to a private office farther back. The space had been stripped of furniture when the last owners of the building had pulled out ahead of the increasing violence and the brutal Russian air force. There were no pictures on the walls, no furniture or filing cabinets set up. Overhead, exposed wiring hung down like snakes from a ceiling stripped bare of light fixtures.

Bodies lay scattered around the room. In the heat sensitive night-vision goggles, the walls looked as if they had been splattered with florescent paint from the spilled blood. The reek of cordite was overwhelming in the tightly confined space. Spent shell casings pressed up against Bolan's feet as he moved through the room. Four corpses were tossed with careless abandon around the enclosure.

More of the folding stock AKS-74s lay in hands quickly cooling in death. The office was a stinking abattoir filled with the stench of torn flesh and the copper tang of pooling blood. Bolan kept his eyes trained on the doorway leading into the inner recesses of the suite. His recon had revealed a surprising turn of events. It was time to adapt, to improvise, to overcome. Carefully, Bolan crouched. He secured an assault rifle by its pistol grip, tugging it free from its owner's dead fingers.

Tucking the skeletal buttstock into his hip, Bolan ensured the safety was disengaged. Once outfitted, he holstered his Glock 17. Safely putting his pistol away freed his hands, and Bolan snapped down the folding stock of the paratrooper carbine to make it more manageable in the enclosed environment. Things were ugly now. The Executioner had been thrown a bloody curve ball, and he was determined to take it in stride.

There was an infrared penlight built into the goggles. When activated, it was like a flashlight in the lenses of the night-vision device, visible only in the infrared spectrum. Using it, Bolan quickly determined that Garabend was not one of the dead.

The soldier stood, slowly unfolding from the crouch he had used to navigate the room. The soles of his boots were tacky with blood. Keeping the AKS tight against his torso, he padded toward the door to the inner office.

Behind the office door came the end of the line. Secrecy and stealth became superfluous the instant he crossed through that final door. Bolan had every reason to suspect that he would find the corpse of Enzik Garabend inside. What he was less certain of, given the freshness of the kills, was whether or not he would find Garabend's murderer in there as well.

Standing at an angle by the office door, Bolan surveyed it as carefully as he could through his NVGs. The door was closed. That seemed wrong. Once the target had been taken out, and considering the mess in the outer chamber, why go to the trouble of carefully closing a door behind you as you left?

The Executioner made his decision. Stepping forward, he raised up high on the ball of one foot and brought his right knee up to his chest where he held the AKS at port arms. Exhaling sharply through his nose, Bolan snapped his curled leg out with explosive power. He thrust through on the breaching kick, his big foot slamming into the door just inside of the handle, even to where the bolt ran in the lock housing.

The door popped open under the sharp force and swung wildly back. Bolan recoiled to one side in an attempt to avoid any returning fire from inside the room. After a heartbeat he tucked in behind the muzzle of his appropriated AKS and moved rapidly through the entrance. He swept the rifle muzzle around as he entered the room, his feet moving in a shuffling motion. His eyes sought the parameters of the room, seeing the contents of the chamber in terms first of motion, second in broad details of shape. He felt a breeze on his face, smelled the damp pollution stink of the Sunzha River bisecting Grozny.

A large desk dominated the middle of the room, a dark hulk in his goggles. The top of it glowed with a dripping luminescence. Behind the desk a body cooled as the night breeze blew in through a window blown to shards. Moving carefully, his nerves crackling with the electricity of potential danger, Bolan checked the corpse.

He reached down and unceremoniously yanked the dangling head up by a shock of greasy hair. In the IR enhancement light, the bland features of Enzik Garabend looked back up at him. The middle-aged man's eyes bulged sightless from his death-slackened face. Bloody holes the size of coins riddled the man's chest, ruining an expensive suit under a waterproof parka.

Bolan was too late.

Disgusted, he put a boot on the edge of the office chair and kicked it over in frustration. It slid a few inches and then toppled. The heavy, loose form of Garabend's body slipped onto the floor with all the deftness of a sopping wet bag of cement. Out of professional habit, he quickly looked around on the floor for Garabend's laptop, or any other effects. Nothing. The place had been stripped clean of all but the ex-terrorist's corpse.

Now that he was sure of Garabend's fate, Bolan knew he had to exit the scene as quickly as possible. The abandoned factory had become red hot. Too hot for a foreigner packing a military arsenal on Russian soil in a time of heightened attacks by a savage, determined insurgency. He had to get out of there, retreat to his safehouse and contact Brognola for extraction.

Suddenly Bolan froze. Some faint sound, almost inaudible on the periphery of his hearing, came to him. He cocked his head to the side, tense.

He couldn't recapture the sound again, now that he was actively listening. In the graveyard silence that surrounded him, Bolan couldn't be sure he'd heard anything to begin with. It was unsettling. The Executioner didn't spook. He slowly sank onto one knee by the sprawled corpse of the Armenian terror merchant and ran an expert hand over the man's body, fishing through his pockets.

Nothing.

Bolan turned and stood. It was then that the necessary angle of vision was correct. The battery light from Garabend's satellite phone burned green, suddenly obvious in the gloomy room. Bolan frowned, head cocked, listening for any sound coming from outside the office. He heard nothing to give him pause and turned his attention back to the sat phone. Garabend's phone was a good catch, not the same as his laptop, to be sure, but still good. It seemed hard to believe that professional operators capable of a hit of this magnitude could have possibly missed it.

Still, though the takedown had all the earmarks of top-line training, Bolan figured it couldn't have been Russian Spesnaz teams. The entire site would have been locked down for the entry team. Intelligence technicians would have been crawling across the site postaction, searching for any evidence. Garabend's bullet riddled corpse would have been whisked away and paraded on Russian television. After the Belsan school siege, dead terrorists made for great ratings from an angry, vengeance minded Russian nation.

Whoever had taken out Garabend had been a player; but not official Russian. Bolan picked up the phone. It was sticky with the dead man's blood. Bolan powered the device off and placed it in a pocket of his nightsuit. The phone provided a clue, in and of itself. The high-tech devices made doing business in the modern age much, much easier, especially from remote or uncivilized areas, but they were a liability as well.

Worldwide, terrorists had learned a lesson a decade earlier, in the spring of 1996, from the death of Dzokhar Dudayev. The Chechen leader had known he needed to limit the time he spent using the satellite phone given to him by his Islamic allies in Turkey. The survivor of two Russian assassination attempts had been wary of Moscow's ability to home in on his communication signal and thus his location.

But on the evening of April 21, Dudayev, baited by Russian President Boris Yeltsin's offer of peace talks, called an adviser in Moscow to discuss the impending negotiations.

Dudayev stayed on the phone too long.

American spy satellites, trained on Iraq and Kuwait, were quickly turned north to the Caucasus Mountains and Chechnya, according to media reports by a former communications specialist with the U.S. National Security Agency—NSA— The satellites pinpointed the Chechen leader's location to within feet of his satellite phone signal, and the coordinates were sent to a Russian fighter jet.

Dudayev was killed by two laser-guided air-to-surface missiles while still holding the phone that had pinpointed his location.

Had Garabend made the same mistake? Only instead of missiles, had a call he made triggered a hit squad or some lone, hyper-skilled, assassin? Whatever the case, Bolan had enough to go on for the moment. Once Aaron "the Bear" Kurtzman and his team got hold of the information in the communication device, they would have plenty of clues for further operations.

Bolan stepped around the desk and moved through the open door into the outer office chamber. The bodies of the dead Armenian's bodyguards still lay sprawled around in haphazard disarray. After years of experience, Bolan had a critical, almost gifted, eye for crime-scene forensics. He was able to recreate the events of even the most horrific battle by the position of corpses, spent shell casings and blood spatter. In this case, rushed for time, he was unable to conclude whether this butcher's work had been done by a coordinated team or a single, talented professional.

Bolan moved carefully through the room. He held his AKS at the ready as he approached the door. His feeling of disquiet had not subsided. He couldn't place his unease, and that made it all the more bothersome. He stalked forward, pausing at the door leading out into the hall.

He stopped, sensed nothing, moved forward.

All hell broke loose.

3

When he stepped through the door and entered the hall, Bolan felt as if he had moved into a field of static electricity. The hair on his arms and the back of his neck lifted straight up as cold squirts of adrenaline surged into his body. The night fighter reacted instantly, without conscious thought. He dropped to one knee and leaned back in the doorway, sweeping the barrel of his AKS up and triggering a blast.

The unmistakable pneumatic cough of a sound-suppressed weapon firing full-automatic assaulted Bolan's ears across the short distance. Shell casings clattered onto the linoleum floor, mixing with the sound of a weapon bolt leveraging back and forth rapidly. Bolan felt the angry whine of bullets fill the space where his head and chest had been only a heartbeat before.

The Executioner targeted diagonally across and down the office hall, firing his Russian assault rifle with practiced, instinctive ease. He let the recoil of the carbine shuttering in his strong grip carry him back through the doorway behind him in a tight roll. From his belly Bolan thrust the muzzle around the doorjamb and arced the weapon back and forth as he laid down quick, suppressive blasts.

The 5.45 mm rounds were deafening in the confined space and his ears rang painfully from the noise. Bolan reached up and jerked his night-vision goggles down so that they dangled from the rubber strap around his neck. He heard the bullets from his assailant's answering burst smack into the plasterboard of the outer wall with smacks that rang louder than the muzzle-braked weapon's own firing cycle.

From the impacts, Bolan determined the shooter was using a submachine gun and not an assault rifle, though he was hard-pressed to identify caliber with the suppressor in use. Bolan scrambled backward and rested his rifle barrel across the still-warm corpse of a dead bodyguard. If there was more than one assassin out there, and he were determined to get him, the person would either fire and maneuver to breach the room door, or possibly use grenades to clear him out.

There was silence for a long moment. Bolan's head raced through strategies and options. If the assassin's intent had been escape, then why had he bothered to stay behind or try to take Bolan out? If the unknown assailant was armed for a quiet kill, then that would indicate he was probably not carrying ordnance much heavier than the silenced submachine gun being used.

The main thing, Bolan's experience told him, was getting momentum back into his possession. He quickly stripped an extra rifle from a dead bodyguard and hooked the sling over his shoulder. Conscious of how vulnerable he was, Bolan crawled back toward the door. He maneuvered the barrel of his AKS through the entrance and triggered an exploratory blast, conducting a recon by fire. Precious seconds ticked away.

Almost immediately, Bolan's aggressive burst was answered with a tightly controlled one. Bullets tore into the wooden door frame and broke up the floor in front of his weapon. Bolan ducked back. He had what he needed. He had found a way to exploit his heavier armament.

The gunman had taken position across and two doors down the hall from the room where Bolan was trapped. From that location the gunmen controlled the fields of fire up and down the hall, preventing Bolan from leaving the office without exposing himself to withering, short-range fire.

Again, Bolan triggered a long, ragged blast. He tore apart the door of the office directly opposite him, then ran his larger caliber rounds down the hall to pour a flurry of lead through the sniper's door. Tracer fire lit up the hallway with surrealistic strips of light like laser blasts in some low-budget science-fiction movie. Bolan could smell his own sweat and the hot oil of his AKS-74. The heavy dust hanging in the air, kicked up by the automatic weapon fire, choked him.

Bolan ducked back around as the gunman triggered an answering burst. Bolan heard the smaller caliber rounds strike the wall outside his door, saw how they failed to penetrate the building materials. It confirmed his suspicions that he was facing no more than a 9 mm caliber in the killer's weapon.

Bolan snarled, gathering himself, and thrust his weapon out the office door a final time. He triggered the AKS and the assault rifle bucked in his hands. Bolan sprinted out through the doorway hard behind his covering fire. His rounds fell like sledgehammers around the door to the room of his ambusher. Hot gases warmed his wrists as the bolt of his weapon snapped open and shut, open and shut, as he carried his burst out to improbable length even as he raced forward.

Two steps from the office door directly opposite Garabend's death room, Bolan's magazine ran dry and the bolt locked open. Without hesitation, he flung down the empty weapon and dived forward. The big man's hard shoulder struck the door. Already riddled with 5.45 mm bullets, the flimsy construction was no match for Bolan's heavy frame and he burst through it into the room.

The Executioner went down with his forward momentum, landing on the shoulder he had used as a battering ram and somersaulting over it smoothly. He came up on one knee and swung his second AKS carbine off his shoulder, leveling it at the wall separating his position from the gunman's. Bolan triggered his weapon from the waist, raking it back and forth in a tight, low Z-pattern. The battlefield rounds chewed through plywood, drywall and insulation with ease, bursting out the other side with terminal velocity.

Still firing, Bolan smoothly uncoiled out of his combat crouch, keeping the arc of his weapon angled downward to better catch an enemy likely pinned against the floor. His intentions were merciless. Momentum, and an attacker's aggression, were with Bolan now, on him like a fugue. Coming to his feet, he shifted the AKS pistol grip from his right to his left hand. His magazine came up dry as he shifted his weight back toward the shattered door to the room.

The handle of Bolan's Glock 17 filled the palm of his free hand as he fired the last rounds through the looted AKS. He was moving, lethally graceful, back out the door to the room, his feet engaged through a complicated series of steps. Out in the hall, smoke from weapons fire and dust billowed in the already gloomy hall.

Bolan stepped out long and lunged forward, sinking to one knee as he came to the edge of his ambusher's door. He made no attempt to slow his momentum but instead let it carry him down to the floor. He breached the edge of the enemy door, letting the barrel of the Glock 17 pistol lead the way. He caught the image of a dark-clad form sprawled out on the floor of the room.

The 9 mm pistol coughed in a double tap, catching the downed figure in the shoulder and head. Blood splashed up and the figure's skull mushroomed out, snapping rudely to the side on a slack neck. A chunk of cottage-cheeselike material splattered out and struck a section of bullet riddled wall.

Bolan popped up, returned to his feet. He moved into the room, weapon poised, ready to react to even the slightest motion or perceived movement. After the frenzied action and brutal cacophony of the gun battle, the sudden return of silence and still felt deafening, almost oppressive. Approaching the dead man, Bolan narrowed his eyes, trying to quickly take in details. Muzzle-flash had ruined his night vision.

Frustrated, Bolan dragged his NVGs back into position and turned on the infrared penlight. The room returned to view in the familiar monochromatic greenish tint. Bolan looked over at the dead gunman's weapon. From the unique silhouette he recognized the subgun as a PP-19 Bizon. Built on a shortened AKS-74 receiver, it had the signature cylindrical high-capacity magazine attached under the fore grip and the AKS folding buttstock. The weapon was usually associated with Russian federal police or army troops, but international arms merchants had been turning up with them more and more as the Russian economy went through its series of shortfalls.

Bolan rolled the man over. Any hopes for identification were gone. The man's face held all the structural integrity of mush. Bolan could easily see the man's thick, tangled beard, however. One of Garabend's bodyguards who had survived the attack?

Bolan knew he didn't have a lot of time. In a city locked down under martial law, the sound of the assault rifle he had been forced to use would draw unwanted attention very quickly. Bolan patted the dead man down. He found a leather wallet filled with Russian bank notes but devoid of identification.

The soldier pulled a thin, flat-faced digital camera from one of the carriers on his harness. He clicked off the IR light and settled his goggles on his forehead. He turned the camera on and opened the lens protector. Without preamble he grabbed the doughy-fleshed hand of the dead man by his index finger. Cradling the camera securely in his palm, Bolan rolled the man's finger across the lens facing of the camera as carefully as any police desk sergeant at a big city precinct house.

Bolan held up the camera, letting the dead killer's hand drop unceremoniously. It struck the bare floor with a dull clap. Bolan pointed the camera at a blank stretch of wall unmarred by his penetrating gunfire. He closed his eyes against the flash and snapped a picture. Later, he would download the snapshot and send it back to Barbara Price, mission controller at Stony Man Farm, for analysis. If the shooter was a bodyguard, that was fine. If he was something else, then Bolan needed to know.

He stood and put the camera away. He grabbed his Glock. It was time to go. Past time.

Bolan's forward operating station in Grozny was an old CIA operations safehouse left over from the Chechen conflicts. Maintained as part of a Global Deployment Readiness Plan by the Operations Division, the residence was little used but constantly prepped. It provided stripped down, untraceable tools for Western intelligence operatives who found themselves working outside of normal geographical station mandates.

Working outside of normal geographical station mandates was something Mack Bolan knew all about.

Upon returning to the house Bolan immediately downloaded the picture of the dead assassin's fingerprint and e-mailed it through an encrypted, anonymous server along with a brief sitrep, to a Stony Man capable site. Aaron Kurtzman would access all federal and international databanks in an effort to find a match.

Bolan drank a beer and made himself a sandwich from the pickings in the refrigerator. He surveyed his surroundings from every window in the place, looked in closets and behind closed doors until he felt like he knew the layout of the place well enough to navigate it in the dark, under fire if need be. He'd made the decision to delay his extraction until Hal Brognola and the

Stony Man team could reconfigure operational alternatives based on the changed situation.

Jack Grimaldi was poised to infiltrate Grozny from a merchant ship anchored in the Caspian. The ship was run under a triple sponsor program combining Naval Intelligence, the Defense Intelligence Agency and the CIA. All offices were coordinated by the post 9/11 Director of National Intelligence office. Task Force 280, as it was coded, provided civilian-use cover of ocean-based assets for government operations. Brognola had managed to insert the veteran Stony Man pilot into the group with a minimum of fuss.

Bolan paced, calm, but filled with a pent-up energy left over from his confrontation with the assassin. Across the room, where he had left it on the table while fixing himself something to eat, his sat phone began to buzz.

Bolan crossed the room quickly and picked it up. He instantly recognized the gruff voice of Hal Brognola on the other end of the encrypted line. The soldier walked over and looked out the window at the quiet residential street from behind the window blinds. He turned his back on the scene and stepped farther into the old house.

"Striker?" Brognola asked.

"Go ahead," Bolan answered.

"You safe? Things quiet?"

"For now. What do you have?"

"I've got a whole bunch of questions and not too many answers," the big Fed said.

"You manage to get an ID off that print I sent you?"

"Oh, yeah. Sure did. We have a situation. The DNI has reacted to the intelligence and asked me to intervene in the matter."

"What problem would this be?"

"The print you got off the shooter came back to one Andre Nicolov, former GRU commando."

"Okay, so he was with the Main Intelligence Directorate. Lots of ex-military types run for-profit ops these days," Bolan said.

"Problem is, this guy is known to be the chief operator for a player known as Sable, also ex-GRU, ex-SVR and now a freelance information broker. Sable has been the source of a CIA counterintelligence operation in Grozny. A consortium of ex-Soviet physicists and various research scientists of Chechen ethnicity opened a think tank group called the Caucasus Data Institute. The SVR, among others, was hot to get their hands on what they were cooking up. The CIA approached them undercover as a private firm about security in an effort to get our fingers into the pie."

"How does Sable fit into this?"

"She ran a surveillance and procurement operation against the institute. By all accounts, the most successful one. She was always one step ahead of Grozny Station."

"She?" Bolan said. "Go on."

"Last year a field officer named Sanders was put on the case. He began making some headway, running stringers, planting misinformation, that sort of thing. Apparently, about two weeks ago, Sable went to Sanders and stated she wanted to explore life in the Federal Witness Protection Program. As a millionaire."

Bolan let a low, appreciative whistle. "Audacious. Her intel that good?"

"Langley thought so. Only there was a problem."

"What's new?"

"Exactly. Sanders went around his chain of command at Grozny Station to alert the agency to the deal. He used an open channel, not the secure lines at the covert house. Immediately after making the call he disappeared and is still missing."

"What do they want me to do?" Bolan asked.

"Sanders had set procedures for irregular contacts. Since you're on the ground, we want you to try to meet with Sanders. Failing that, follow up on anything you can shake loose."

"Should be a piece of cake," Bolan said dryly.

"I know, Striker," Brognola answered. "But there's an operative out there who may be in trouble and a treasure trove of information that could be damaging to the U.S. if it falls into the wrong hands."

"Sable?"

"Sable," Brognola agreed. "We think she has Garabend's laptop now."

"I'm a shooter, not a spy. You know that, Hal."

"This is Chechnya, Striker, you can't be anything *but* a shooter and expect to make headway."

"All right, tell me everything I need to know."

5

Bolan entered The Berliner casino.

The place was full, but not crowded, and he heard the spinning of roulette wheels and the dissonance of slot machines over the more general noise of the crowd.

Bolan gazed across the crowd. He kept his thoughts as unfocused and bland as the neutral expression on his face. He wasn't looking for anything specific, he was simply soaking in details, waiting to see if his inner radar picked up any blips. He surveyed the casino from payout cage to bar, then from security desk to the table games.

The guards Bolan saw looked hard. It was easy to come by veteran killers in Chechnya, though the real hard cases drifted into the heavily ex-military Russian syndicates. He saw a fat man with two blondes—each supporting improbably large breast implants—on each of his arms. He saw a nervous-looking Asian man puffing away on a cigarette as the dealer turned over cards and took his chips. A broad-shouldered guy with a crew cut leaned against an elegantly decorated pillar fiddling with a gold bracelet.

The Berliner casino was a strange mix, influenced by the youth club in the basement of the property as well as the gaming floor. Wealthy clients mixed with the partygoers, young and old. The place was neither a dive nor too high end. There was a fair mix of Westerners in the crowd. Bolan nodded to himself. It was a good establishment to go unnoticed in, and he understood why Sanders had chosen it as a drop point and meet place.

Bolan walked over to the bar. He watched pretty girls in revealing dresses or the sexy cocktail waitresses as a cover for his perpetual surveillance. He ordered a beer in a pint glass, left the bartender a tip and took his beer to the casino cage where he changed some cash into chips with the help of a brunette in a low cut uniform and too much eye shadow.

The soldier shook his chips loosely in his hand and strolled toward the roulette table. He knew roulette was a sucker's bet, but he'd do it the way Sanders wanted.

As Bolan approached the table, he idly second-guessed himself, wondering if his decision to come unarmed was wise. He was still operating under his journalist cover and a weapons charge by overzealous police troops could unravel the whole operation at this point.

Bolan eased up to the table and made eye contact with the croupier before putting the equivalent of a twenty-five-dollar token on Black 8.

Barbara Price had informed him of the Agency's covert station house location in the Grozny downtown where he could make contact and get equipment as he needed. Bolan had chosen to bypass ordinary channels, at least initially.

Sanders had made his call from an emergency drop cutout phone and not from the Grozny to Moscow station line. There had been no explanation for this irregularity, and Bolan had chosen to follow Sanders's lead in avoiding usual channels. Bolan's paranoia was omnidirectional and hard earned.

The croupier called Red 23 the winner and took Bolan's money. The soldier slid another chip onto Black 8 to replace the one he'd lost. The big-shouldered guy with the crew cut wandered over to watch the wheel. The fat man said something, and the two blondes barked laughter like trained seals. The wheel spun and the white ball jumped and bounced its way across the device. After a moment the ball settled into one of the slots and the croupier called Red 11 the winner.

Bolan had to admit the casino protocol was a wise set up despite the seeming cinematic feel of the practice. Someone could remain anonymous in the crowd, surveying the environment. The contact would make no discernible moves that threatened exposure if he was under surveillance. Either party could simply walk from the scene without commotion if something seemed askew.

The Executioner eyed his watch, then slid another chip onto Black 8. He almost wanted to place another bet, just to make things interesting, but he was afraid the diversity could potentially throw off his contact. Sanders didn't know him by sight, so any variation from the established contact routine would be stupid. The Asian man, eyes glassy, left the blackjack dealer and stumbled up to the table as Bolan lost again. Two security guards in ill-fitting jackets watched, seemingly bored. They were joined by a third after a moment.

Bolan put his chip down on Black 8 again. The guy with the crew cut ordered a drink from a passing cocktail waitress. The Asian man changed Russian rubles into chips at the table and lit another cigarette. One of the blondes had moved behind the fat man and was whispering into his ear while she pressed her breasts against his back. The other woman leaned in beside him, hand in his lap under the table as he played.

"Red 4," the dealer said.

Bolan put his chip on Black 8, once more.

"Final time," he said in passable Russian.

There was a tense moment when the Asian man began throwing chips across the board, but he didn't play Black 8 and Bolan relaxed as the croupier called an end to bets.

This was it, Bolan reflected. The time for the meet in the prescribed manner was past. Sanders hadn't shown. It was official. Grozny was a problem.

Bolan watched the roulette ball bounce around the revolving wheel. As he watched it hit Green 00, nothing obvious had changed, but he smelled danger.

Throwing a chip down for the croupier, Bolan rose.

It seemed he could feel the weight of the sniper's crosshairs on his exposed back, even though he knew that was ridiculous. Sanders hadn't shown, but that didn't necessarily mean the meet location had been compromised.

Bolan was sure Sanders was in trouble. He was sitting on a top-level asset itching to defect. He had avoided his station command, used asymmetrical communications and had missed a last chance emergency meet. Bolan frowned as he walked. Something wasn't right.

He walked outside and flipped open his regular cell phone. He hit a number on his speed dial while hailing a taxi driver in a battered old Volvo. When the connection was made, he spoke briefly into the phone.

"Black 8 was a bust, stage two."

Bolan hung up the phone, his cell line was open, and he'd relied upon brevity and obtuse langue for security.

Such a protocol was better than getting caught in the open with a military satellite phone. Bolan climbed into the taxi.

BOLAN STUFFED HIS HANDS inside the pockets of his jacket and headed into the train station. The very last of the workday commuters were going home, and the old building was clearing out quickly as he entered. He wove his way through the thinning crowd, pushing away from the passenger areas and toward the freight docks.

Wire crates stuffed with chickens were set against the one wall. The smell of animals was strong. Bolan noted the hardy determination of the people in this war zone to continue on with their lives. He had seen it across the globe, but it never failed to give him hope for the human condition.

Bolan got lost in the crowd, then turned back the way he'd come, exiting the building. He cut through dank alleys and dodged across busy streets until he'd made it about two blocks away from the central train station.

He stopped in front of a window display filled with pictures of women in school uniforms being spanked or tied up. His eyes scanned the window, attempting to survey the street behind him in the reflection. The light was too bad for that, so he entered the porn shop.

The inside of the shop was illuminated with garish light from neon tubes. Skin magazines and the box covers for movies were stuffed into cheap racks. A section on the far wall was filled with various sexual devices and toys. The main room was filled with furtive-eyed men who avoided any contact with one another.

Bolan walked through the store, ignoring the other patrons. He entered the gloomy mouth to the hall where the peep shows were located. He could hear gasps and moans coming from behind the closed doors to the video monitor booths. He heard the slap of a hand on flesh and women's cries—some in faux pleasure, many in pain. He moved past the doors. The layout for the coin-operated theaters was in a T-shaped hallway. He walked down the long leg of the T past the video booths.

Along the back wall were the live-show booths. He turned left at the juncture and went to the second to last door. An out-of-date pop song was blasting through a cheap stereo system. The light above the booth door showed red, indicating it was occupied.

The Executioner waited. After a few moments the song changed and a disheveled looking middle-aged man in a suit scurried out. He almost ran into Bolan and squeaked guiltily. He looked up, eyes appearing enormous behind thick glasses.

Bolan snarled down at him and the man hurried out of the hall.

The cramped booth stunk, and Bolan looked around, disgust on his face now that he was alone. He shoved the bolt on the door home, then fed a few coins into the wall slot to change the light outside to red.

A narrow opening slid back and, through smeary glass, Bolan caught a glimpse of a nude woman in a room surrounded by coin-operated windows. Bolan reached into his pocket and pulled a credit card from his wallet. He turned away from the window and squatted.

Using the edge of the credit card to spare his fingers any unpleasant contact, Bolan reached up under the seat mounted in the wall. The booth was known to be Sanders's blind drop. He'd been running stringers in his surveillance operation against the institute and picking up hard copy materials from them in this booth.

Bolan paused as he felt his card touch something other than the wooden underside of the filthy little bench. He reached under the seat and immediately frowned. Sanders had attached a thin metal sleeve to hold items and the drop was stuffed full of papers.

In undercover intelligence work, drops were made in public places to explain movement patterns to unfriendly surveillance. They weren't meant to be cache points. There was seldom longer than an hour between delivery and retrieval at such points, nor was one site usually meant for more than a single stringer.

Bolan slid out five manila envelopes of varying thickness. He knew things were bad. Operational security was dissolving all around him. He stood and slid the envelopes into the inside pocket of his leather jacket. He needed to get out and away from the drop site. He had to assume he was made. That didn't necessarily mean the operation was over. He decided that if he needed to do open source or interview-based investigations, then it was still better for him to do it than risk the cover of another operative.

He wasn't going to make it easy for the opposition, however.

Bolan unlocked the door to the booth and stepped out into the gloomy hallway. He sensed movement at the intersection of the theatre hall and looked up. The broad-shouldered man with the crew cut from the casino rounded the corner. Their eyes met, locked in recognition.

The soldier didn't believe in coincidences. He couldn't believe in them and continue to survive in a covert operations environment. He launched himself instantly, driving straight at the man, using his momentum to rise off the ground, swinging his right knee up. He drove his knee hard into the man's ribs. The guy grunted and staggered backward from the impact.

Bolan landed and swept his hands up to grip the back of the man's head in a maneuver designed to control him. The man's reflexes were lightening quick, and he struck the inside of Bolan's right arm at the nerve cluster just behind the elbow. Pain flashed up the Executioner's arm and it was knocked aside, leaving an opening.

The crew cut man stepped forward and struck Bolan with a fist to his exposed ribs. The big American stumbled, bruised, hurt and surprised. He brought his arms up in front of him and instinctively turned to the side and raised a leg to ward off further blows.

Instead of pushing his advantage physically, the man from the casino shuffled backward and his right hand went for the small of his back. Bolan saw the movement and moved forward. The man's hands reappeared holding a flat, black automatic pistol.

The Executioner stepped forward, moving to the outside of the muscled killer's arm. The tight space of the hallway hampered his movements, slowing him. He twisted so that he faced the man at a nearly ninety-degree angle. Bolan's left hand caught his adversary's wrist just behind the pistol and, using the man's own forward motion, pulled him off balance. Bolan used his right hand to snap a straight punch into his opponent's temple.

The impact was loud in the confined space, and the man sagged under the sharp force. Bolan stepped away, twisting at the hips. The hand that had just delivered the brutal punch twisted to became a claw, sweeping the man's head backward while Bolan pulled the gun hand back and thrust his chest out against the trapped arm, over extending the elbow.

The gun clattered to the floor and the man dropped as well. Without thinking, operating on instinct, Bolan lifted his foot and drove his heel straight down into the man's throat. The killer's eyes startled open wide, then slid upward into his head.

Bolan moved quickly. He glanced around him and saw no one. The altercation had lasted only heartbeats, and the computerized music system still blared out the same song. Bolan knelt and slid the man's pistol into the small of his back before expertly patting down the body.

He pulled out a wallet, a cell phone and a knife. Bolan pocketed the items and stood. He smoothed down the front of his jacket over the bulge made by the envelopes from Sanders's drop point. He held his head up and coolly walked out of the dark hallway.

Bolan's nerves were on fire as he made his way for the door. He had no intention of being in the building when the body was found. He pushed through the door and out into the street. He looked around carefully. The point man might have had backup.

The soldier started walking, looking for a taxi. It was possible the man had been assigned surveillance and had decided to take Bolan out on his own. If he was a Russian stringer, then it was even possible he had been working alone on a "zone defense" surveillance. Bolan had no intention of taking that possibility for granted, however.

He needed to get to his safehouse and take stock of what he'd learned since hitting the ground in Chechnya, just four hours earlier. Bolan pushed his way through a lively crowd as he looked for a taxi. He didn't see one, and he decided to head back toward the train station. He'd have his choice of taxis there, and the walk would give him a chance to shake out anyone shadowing him.

He crossed the busy strip, ignoring angry shouts and beeping horns. Such things were commonplace. This section of the city stank, and the cold, seasonal damp made him feel like his skin was covered in a greasy film. Reaching the other side of the street, Bolan ducked into the alley he'd used to reach the porn shop.

He stepped passed an unconscious man sprawled in the mouth of the alley. The man reeked of strong, cheap booze. Bolan entered alley, his nostrils flaring at the stench of rotting garbage and piles of refuse. Halfway down the alley he turned to look over his shoulder. No preternatural combat sense had warned him, just good tradecraft. A simple matter of being careful. He saw a silhouette enter the alley and he spun, dropping to one knee. He pulled his pistol free and crouched.

The figure at the end of the alley already had his pistol out and it barked twice. Two rounds buzzed through the air above Bolan's head, just where his heart would have been were he still standing. He answered with a trio of 9 mm rounds.

His vision was blurred by the blinding flash of the weapon and his ears buzzed from the sudden, sharp reports. At the end of the alley he had a sense of a figure spinning away. He heard the sleeping man shout in surprise and saw him sit up.

Realizing that the figure was going for the cover of the building edge, Bolan popped up and shuffled quickly backward. The figure came around the edge of the alley and got off a hasty shot that sang wide. Bolan answered with a single shot designed to impact the wall near the figure's head and spray chips. His round drove the gunman back behind cover and Bolan took his opportunity to escape out of the alley.

The Executioner hit the street running, shouldering his way through the crowd like a running back pushing for open field. He knocked several pedestrians to the ground, ignoring their cries of outrage.

He reached the front of the train station and jogged over to the line of waiting taxis, leaned forward and pushed some folded bills into the driver's waiting hand. He rattled off an address to get the man moving and leaned back into the ratty seat as the driver pulled out into traffic.

The pistol was warm against the small of his back and its weight was reassuring. Finally the taxi driver made it out into the heavy traffic and Bolan allowed himself to relax. The driver said something at him in what he thought was a Georgian accent, and Bolan responded in colloquial Russian.

He reached into his jacket and felt the envelopes there. Brognola wasn't going to be happy about this.

The town house was in an upscale, international resident section of the city, adjacent to the old financial district. Bolan had the taxi driver drop him a couple of blocks away, and he approached from the rear making use of the clean, wide alleys running between the houses.

It was a quiet neighborhood, and Bolan didn't notice anyone up and moving about at such a late hour. It was place of good security due to the high concentration of foreign businessmen from the petroleum and mining industries. People here, Bolan knew, lived a hell of a lot better than they did in the rest of the Grozny metropolis.

At the back gate Bolan punched the code Barbara Price had given him into the keypad hidden behind a false plaque and disabled the alarm system. He entered the little walkway and shut the gate tightly behind him. At the back door of the safehouse, Bolan tipped up a bird feeder hanging from a low tree branch and got the key to the dead-bolt lock.

Once inside the two-story house he locked the door behind him and reengaged the alarm system. He went into the Western-style kitchen and pulled open the fridge door. The fridge was well stocked, and he pulled out a bright red Coca-Cola can. He leaned against the counter, guzzled the soda and tossed the empty can into the nearby garbage bin.

Bolan pulled the envelopes free of his jacket pocket and threw them on the kitchen table. He removed the handgun from the small of his back and set it next to the envelopes. He took off his jacket and sat down.

Bolan sighed and leaned forward, putting his head in his hands and closing his eyes for a moment. His knuckles were still slightly sore from where they'd struck the man in the porn shop.

After a moment he pulled the first of the five manila envelopes over to him. He reached behind him and drew the knife he had taken from the man he'd killed. He opened the folding handles with practiced flicks of his wrist, then used the knife blade to open the first envelope.

Inside Bolan found computer printouts. He shifted them around, studying the details. It was a schematic diagram. He frowned, knowing he didn't have the technical expertise to know what the blueprints showed. Perhaps they were the electronics to the guidance systems DNI had been so worried Sable had procured. Perhaps they were something else.

Bolan pushed the schematic printout aside and opened up the next envelope. It contained more of the same. The third one showed a list of numbers running down a spreadsheet. He knew he was looking at an accounting ledger. The numbers showed transactions, dates, amounts and specific account numbers.

"You were getting some good stuff," Bolan murmured to the absent Sanders.

He threw the papers on top of the pile of information, set the knife on the table and rubbed his eyes. He breathed deeply.

He picked up the next to the last envelope and opened it quickly. Several photos spilled out across the desk. He sat up, suddenly alert, completely surprised by what he was seeing.

In the photos two women were locked together, naked, on a bed. Bolan held them up. It showed a pretty, younger Asian woman kissing a blond woman. The Asian was attractive, but the blonde had an icy beauty, as hard as diamonds, that Bolan had only seen in expensive call girls.

He looked at the rest of the pictures. The women, already naked, progressed quickly beyond the kissing stage. In one shot the brunette had her face buried between the blonde's smooth thighs. The blonde was looking down on the younger woman, her face haughty as she pulled at the woman's hair.

"What's this all about, Sanders?" Bolan wondered.

Bolan pulled two photos out of the pile and set them in front of him. He slid the rest back into their envelope. The two photos he kept out each showed close shots of the women's faces. Bolan studied them intently, memorizing every detail. When he was satisfied he'd recognize them in person, he put them away and opened the final envelope from the drop.

Inside the envelope was folded piece of stationery. Bolan unfolded it and looked at what was written there. It was a simple series of numbers.

Bolan frowned. If the drop was a fast turnover situation, then it was possible the code was a simple system meant for Sanders to decipher quickly and then destroy, rather than sophisticated encryption.

The soldier got up and stretched. He went back out into the living area where he had seen a desk with a computer on it. It might help with research, but the house had been set up as a hideaway, not a field operations center, and communications were not infallibly secure. There were the cyberequivalents of blind drops, but Bolan had no intention of using them from this location unless absolutely necessary.

Bolan needed a good, down and dirty, field code Sanders might have instructed a stringer in. From the numbers, it seemed to be a replacement code of some sort. Bolan got to work with pen and paper. He was in Operational Theater Six. He added that to the last digit of the day of the date of the drop, then transposed the numbers with letters of the alphabet.

He tried the day Sanders had made his call, got a jumble of alphabet letters, then tried switching the letters out with the next letter in the alphabet. Nothing. He tried it with the letter prior and came up empty. He snarled in frustration and thrust the sheets of paper away.

Bolan got up and went to the refrigerator. He reached in and pulled out a green bottle of Heineken. He idly wondered what poor schmuck had gone all the way through college CIA recruitment only to find himself putting his security clearance to use stocking the fridge in some rarely used safehouse.

Bolan sat the beer down unopened. His mind was cluttered with images, snapshot memories of a hundred different events and a thousand different days from his past. He walked over to the doorway and reached up to grab the lip of the frame at the top. He dug his fingers in tightly and began to pull himself up in slow, deliberate movements. The exercise was an old rock climbing movement designed to strengthen the hands and forearms as much as the biceps and back.

After an easy fifteen chin-ups to get his blood moving, Bolan lowered himself and walked back to the table. He clenched and unclenched his fists, loosening the muscles of his grip. He shrugged back to stretch his shoulders and looked down at the table.

Bolan shook random thoughts away and sat, pulling his notes toward him. He looked at the numbers. They sat there, stubbornly refusing to give up their secrets. Then a slow smile slid across his face.

The soldier stood and crossed to the computer where he immediately logged on. He set his notes beside him at the desk and signed on to the Internet. He pulled up a Russian-English dictionary Website. He typed a word from his notes into the computer. The word came back unknown. Bolan threw that sheet down and picked up the sheet where he had transposed the letter corresponding with the number abstraction with the letter directly following it.

He hurriedly typed the series of letters into the computer. He got a match. He wrote the match down, then typed in each word until he translated the note in its entirety. When he was done he leaned back, feeling satisfied despite himself.

He read the note.

Tan is a dupe. Break all contact.

7

Bolan got out of the taxi on a secondary street in Grozny's renovated financial district. The gigantic, gutted structure of the old Oil Ministry building cast long shadows over the Meltzer Import Export Emporium. The covert station house was a tasteful, discreet building with darkened, lead-lined windows and subdued walls.

The soldier surveyed the building. He'd tried to avoid making contact with Grozny station only because Sanders himself had avoided using the place in making contact with higher authority. Bolan would have preferred to slip in and out of this operations region without officially entering the fiefdom of the local station.

But Sanders' failure to show for the meet and subsequent events had made such an approach unworkable. Bolan had no intention of leaving the drop envelopes with them. He'd put them in a safe at the secure house before taking a shower and going to bed.

Bolan entered the austere offices and approached a pretty receptionist behind a massive desk. A plaque on her desk read Ms. Pong, and her face seemed locked in a mask of perpetual boredom. She regarded Bolan with a disinterested stare. He smiled his good morning.

"You speak English?" he asked.

"Of course."

"I have a question about goods."

"Yes?"

"I was wondering if you could tell me whether or not the futures in Chechen oil could be considered robust?"

The receptionist didn't blink at the covert parole code. She stared up at Bolan with expressionless, black eyes. Her voice was monotone when she answered.

"I wouldn't know. We only handle manufactured goods," she said. "Please wait in there."

The receptionist indicated a door set discreetly in the wall toward the back of the lobby, away from the elevator banks and half-hidden by a potted rubber tree plant. She reached a well-manicured hand under her desktop, and a muted buzzer sounded.

Bolan crossed the room quickly and went through the door. He heard an electronically controlled dead bolt slide into place as the door swung closed behind him. He looked around.

He was in a short, well-lit hallway. A line of comfortable chairs sat against a wall decorated in muted tones. Bolan sat, looking for the security cameras. Unable to spot them, he decided they were using telescopic fiber optics.

A door in the hallway opened and a man walked out. Bolan sized him up and didn't like the vibe he picked up. He was Caucasian and big. Big in the way Eastern Europeans and Russians seemed to get as they slipped into middle age. The man stood almost a full head taller than Bolan and had to have weighted in at close to three hundred pounds. He looked like a bear right before hibernation—powerful muscles covered by copious amounts of fat.

The man wore a mustache and beard, shot through with gray, and his hairline receded prodigiously. His suit was expensive-looking, as was his gold watch. He strode up and stopped before Bolan, who had risen at the man's approach.

"You are from the DNI," the man said.

It wasn't a question and he didn't offer to shake hands.

"I already know that. Who are you?" Bolan said calmly.

The man stepped forward into Bolan's space in a maneuver clearly designed to intimidate the newcomer. It was the kind of bluster that occurred every day in boardrooms, but it was a disrespectful move that could get a person killed in a prison yard or the wrong kind of bar.

Bolan stepped into the looming approach and both men stopped within a hairbreadth of butting chests. The man's gut was considerable, but up close he looked strong enough to wrestle tigers. Bolan didn't back down. The pair locked fierce gazes, neither man blinking.

"I see you've met case officer Kubrick," a cultured voice from behind them said.

Bolan's eyes flickered away, and he took in the second man who had just emerged from one of the office doorways. A mousy woman stood behind him, arms hugging a massive pile of folders and paperwork.

"You are here about the Sanders situation, correct?" the new arrival asked.

"Yes," Bolan replied.

Bolan turned and put his shoulder into that of the man identified as Kubrick. He stepped forward, dipping slightly at the knees as he did so. As the Executioner stepped past Kubrick, he rose up and caught the heavier man in the ribs with his shoulder, where he had a leverage advantage. Bolan brushed past the larger man, unbalancing him so that he stumbled.

Kubrick swore, and Bolan turned his back on him as the second man addressed him.

"I am Claus Lich, station principal."

"Matt Cooper," Bolan said, extending his hand.

"That is my director of operations, Herman Kubrick. He's been running the institute case." Lich met Bolan's eyes with his own unaffected gaze. "He'll be your liaison in this matter. Herman?"

"Yes, Mr. Lich?"

Kubrick stepped forward, brushing down the front of his suit where Bolan's nudge had left him disheveled.

"Please show Mr. Cooper every courtesy. Bring him up to speed and then provide him with whatever help we can offer."

Lich turned and ushered the tepid little woman into his open office door ahead of him. He turned back before he followed her in. He looked at Bolan like a lab tech trying to classify a distasteful, but possibly deadly, new strain of virus.

"Cooper." Lich nodded.

Bolan nodded back.

Lich gave Bolan a freezing smile before disappearing into his office. He'd never looked toward Kubrick again after giving his instructions.

Bolan frowned reflectively as he watched the station principal's door bang shut. He turned and looked at Kubrick.

"Well, Herman, we going to get this done?" Bolan said.

"Call me Kubrick, asshole. Follow me."

Kubrick turned and walked toward the end of the hall

where Bolan had entered. He moved fast for such a big man and he didn't look back to see if Bolan was following him.

The Executioner looked impassively at the man's retreating back before relenting and following him. Someone had tried to kill him, and Bolan wasn't going to let macho posturing or turf wars keep him from his mission. Something was wrong in Grozny, and he meant to find out what.

"HOLD MY CALLS," Kubrick said into his cell phone. "Tell them I have a breakfast meeting. I shouldn't be gone long." Kubrick hung up.

"Where are we going?" Bolan asked.

"I'm hungry. I know a place where we won't be interrupted and the help knows how to mind their own business."

"I imagine you know quite a bit about the restaurant scene," Bolan remarked.

"Screw you."

Kubrick navigated Grozny efficiently, using diplomatic credentials to pass quickly through security checkpoints. The Chechen insurgents had, for the most part, been pushed into the Caucasus Mountains and the bulk of combat operations were taking place along the Georgian border.

Bolan looked out the tinted windows of Kubrick's Mercedes. He watched landmarks slide by they drove across the busy, modern streets of the city center. He had a feeling Kubrick didn't spend too much time in the slums or out in the bush.

He and Kubrick were like two bulls in a field and butting heads came naturally to them. Bolan was an interloper on Kubrick's turf, and Lich's for that matter. Bolan had done his homework at the safehouse, and he was nominally well versed in the history of both men.

Lich had come up through the ranks old school. He'd been a logistics officer for Air America operations in the Asian theater during the sixties and had then been assigned to Berlin, running counterintelligence operations against Communist incursions on all levels. He'd made his bones working the iron curtain and he'd stayed there.

Other than that cursory background, Brognola hadn't been able to access Lich's agency file—a fact the big Fed had found very troubling. Lich's background was buried so deep that Bolan, through Brognola, had been frozen out.

Kubrick was a different story. He was a classic Agency success story. He'd combined adequate fieldwork with a talent for playing the sycophant. He'd started out doing interrogation of captured North Korean infiltrators with the Defense Intelligence Agency before getting assigned to Berlin under Lich in the early eighties.

He bounced around playing the role as Lich's number two for decades. Like Lich, he was rumored to have a considerable financial portfolio built using information gleaned during classified operations. The pair of them were known as down and dirty operators who brushed the line often—but as of yet no one had suggested that the duo had actually crossed it.

But Sanders had jeopardized his operational security to place that call from outside of station control.

Bolan mulled it all over while Kubrick drove. After about fifteen minutes they pulled up to a valet parking lot in front of a moderately expensive-looking restaurant in the International District. Such a place was real luxury—in a place like Grozny. A smiling employee in a red suit, took the keys from the massive Kubrick and gave him a paper ticket.

"This is on your expense account, not mine," Bolan said, playing his part, as they entered the restaurant.

Once they were seated and had ordered food and coffee, the game was ready to begin.

"What do you know?" Kubrick demanded.

"I'm here to learn," Bolan said, sidestepping. "Just start at the beginning. Walk me through it like I was a child."

"Not much of a stretch," Kubrick grunted.

"Then it should be easy," Bolan said with a shrug.

Kubrick stared at Bolan for a moment over his plate. His eyes glittered, and he looked as venomous as a pit viper. Bolan bit into a piece of toast and returned Kubrick's glare.

Kubrick relented.

"Sanders claims he's bringing Sable in, that she's turned. I think it's bullshit. I think she's playing that puppy. I've worked counterops against Sable for years now. I was the one who caught her penetration of the institute, Sanders was *my* stringer. I have more experience with this agent than anyone in the Company. Yet when Sanders gets a lead in the case, he fails to contact me. I find that troubling…and so should you, frankly."

"Maybe he doesn't trust you. Maybe Sanders thinks you've gone bad," Bolan said.

He kept his voice deliberate, completely dropping the baiting tone he'd used up until then. He was walking dangerous ground. He watched Kubrick carefully for a reaction. He was disappointed.

"That's the point, Cooper. I thought you troubleshooters were supposed to be savvy operators. If Sander's doesn't trust me, that means Sable *is* playing him. It means he may think she is coming over, but the truth is she's probably working him for everything she can get. She's good, Cooper. She's good."

"How about Tan?" Bolan asked, taking a chance.

Kubrick's tradecraft went right out the window. His face grew red and he dropped his fork onto the table with a disgusted look. He picked up his napkin and dabbed at his mouth where food had caught in his beard.

"How do you know about Tan?" Kubrick demanded.

Bolan shrugged. "Guys talk, you hear things."

"Sylvia Tan works at the Caucasus Data Institute." Kubrick said finally. "She grew up in Taiwan in a fairly affluent family. They sent her away to college. She got a social conscience in college, Berkeley no less, where she studied programming and electronics."

Bolan raised his eyebrows. "Chinese get to her, or the Russians?" he asked.

"First the Russians. Through a Berkeley splinter branch of the California ACLU. Tan joined when she returned home to Taiwan to get her master's. The threat of Uncle Mao hits a little too close to home in Taiwan for even the lunatic fringe to fully embrace them."

The waitress came with the bill and discreetly set it in the exact middle of the table. Bolan smiled fully at the blushing woman and pushed the little red folder toward the burly station officer.

Kubrick frowned, the paid the tab.

"Then she got a job at the institute," Bolan prompted. "She left home and headed here? Just like that?"

"Yeah. There was a hint of scandal. I assume sexual,

but I can't verify it. She bailed out of Taiwan in the nineties. That's all we know. I've had her under observation for a couple of years."

"That much I had," Bolan lied. "How does Sanders fit in?"

"I gave the Tan surveillance to Sanders, as a way to get his feet wet. He surprised me. He got Vesler, the director at the institute, to put him on as a security consultant in addition to his liaison role from the Agency. He began to cultivate Tan. I think she's the one who led him to Sable."

"I'll need to see the files on Vesler, Tan and the institute," Bolan said.

"Fine. I'll call ahead to Ms. Pong and arrange it."

"You're not coming back?" Bolan queried.

"No. I have other matters. Matters that are none of your business."

"Great. You springing for cab fare?" Bolan goaded.

"Look, asshole," Kubrick snapped, rising to the bait. "I don't like you paramilitary cowboys. I don't like outside interference in my operations, and I don't like *you*."

"You don't have to like me, fat man." Bolan answered back. "You just have to make sure I have everything I need to get this job done."

Kubrick rose, and his face was so angry that Bolan thought he'd finally pushed the case officer too hard. He tensed the muscles of his legs to rise and meet Kubrick's attack.

Kubrick made a visible effort to control himself. He reached into the pocket of his suit jacket and removed his valet ticket. He threw it on the table.

"I'll take the cab," he said. "You can take my car to the station. Try to be gone by the time I return."

Pulling out his cell phone, Kubrick turned and stalked out of the restaurant before Bolan could reply. The soldier watched him go, his face impassive. He reached over and picked up the valet ticket. He contemplated it thoughtfully before also rising and making his way out of the restaurant.

Bolan slid behind the wheel of the idling Mercedes after tipping the valet. He pulled the car out into traffic. Bolan knew, given the attempt on his life, that if Sanders had left Kubrick out of the op because of fears his supervisors were dirty, then Bolan had every reason to suspect that Kubrick was setting him up now.

Bolan checked out the interior of the vehicle. The Mercedes was an automatic. To get the best performance out of an automobile, especially under offensive driving situations, a standard transmission, preferably a five speed, was usually best. The CD player held nothing but classical music, heavy on Wagner, light on Chopin.

Bolan eyed his mirrors, reflexively looking for a tail. Kubrick's hostility was something he'd come to expect from case officers. Even the most experienced agents couldn't comprehend the world in which Bolan existed. They often feared what they couldn't understand.

Bolan gunned the automobile through traffic. He didn't think Kubrick—if he was crooked—would do anything so obvious as to plan a hit in his own vehicle. Unless he was going to try to make it look as if the hit were intended for *him*.

Bolan tried to order his thoughts. He'd taken in a lot of information in a very short time. Each bit of information opened up a multitude of possibilities. He needed to itemize and then prioritize that information. He found a station on the radio, turned up the volume. The sound system in the Mercedes was top-notch. His eyes flicked to his rearview mirror.

Bolan surveyed the traffic. He didn't try to concentrate too closely on any one thing or automobile, but instead let his eyes flit across the view, getting a feel for what was behind him. He tried to match up what Kubrick had told him with the briefing he'd been given.

Sanders had been running a flip operation for a freelance ex-Soviet agent, something that would be a gold mine for American intelligence. He'd been working the Grozny Station under Lich, in the field as Kubrick's stringer. He'd managed to somehow bunny hop Sable's stalking horse, Sylvia Tan, and get to Sable herself, a feat Kubrick hadn't been able to manage in more than eight years of covert fencing.

Then, when it was time to bring the prize into the boat, Sanders disappeared. He circumvented his normal chain of command and used unsecured lines to activate the turnover—a turnover he failed to show for. A check of his blind drop revealed an accumulation of sensitive material that Kubrick should have known about and collected. Then someone tried to kill Bolan when he went nosing around.

Bolan snapped out of his reverie. Ahead of him a light at an intersection suddenly turned yellow. He was too close to the light to stop, short of slamming on his brakes. Instead he exercised the Mercedes' big engine and shot through the light and across the avenue. Automatically his eyes found his rearview mirror.

A gunmetal gray Audi cut out from behind a battered old Toyota delivery truck. It slipped around the larger vehicle and shot across the intersection, running a red light and triggering a cacophony of angry horn blasts. The car cut its speed on the other side of the intersection and dropped into traffic about three cars behind Bolan.

The soldier wasn't particularly surprised. He was being tailed. For the Audi to take a risk on such an obvious play as running the red light, he assumed that it was a single shadow and not a team.

Bolan wondered what if it was a legit stringer for Kubrick checking up on the new kid in town. Was it a part of some corruption on Kubrick's or Lich's part? Was it a third party player, perhaps whoever had taken a shot at him near the railway station? Bolan had plenty of questions, but he didn't have any answers.

At the moment the only people with the answers to those questions were in the Audi behind him. Bolan kept his speed down to match the flow of traffic as he crossed the bridge over the river and into one of Grozny's refugee-filled ghettos and one of the largest open-air markets in the Russian republic.

He had intended to head directly back to the Meltzer Emporium to look over the files. He debated with himself over a new, bolder plan. This Sable op was not an intelligence operation, it was a counterintelligence situation. He was not conducting a survey on a known article, but rather was attempting to ferret out an unknown to whom Bolan might already be a very well-established entity.

Bolan considered a method of operation used to jump-start investigations where there were either no leads, or too many. Dubbed the Judas Goat Scenario, it was risky and dismissed as cowboy antics by more austere and reserved operators. Named after the practice of Indian or Kashmir hunters, it was a metaphor for their strategy of using a staked goat to draw whatever tigers were in the area into an ambush.

The operator simply placed himself in the contested environment and announced his presence and intentions. Whoever went after the bait tipped his hand and revealed himself. Bolan needed answers, and he was fortunate enough to know of someone readily available who could answer them.

The driver of the Audi.

Bolan took some time to get into position. He drove carefully, keeping in deep pockets of traffic, stopping for streetlights, driving carefully and defensively. He made every decision opposite to the way a person trying to lose a tail would act. His hope was to lull the Audi driver into complacency. It was imperative that the hunted think he remained the hunter.

Bolan chose his trap as best he could with his limited knowledge of the foreign urban environment. He stayed away from shopping complexes. Those kinds of settings would encourage the shadow to get out of his car and follow Bolan inside, in hopes of observing who the mark met with. Bolan needed something like a restaurant or apartment building where the tail would feel it too risky to do more than survey Bolan's entrance and exit times.

Finally, on the edge of market district, Bolan found a suitable location. High-rise apartments, modern but basic, they lined several streets between the market and the river. They were relatively unmarked by bullets or artillery fire.

Bolan pulled the Mercedes to the curb. He set himself before stepping out and checking the street. Groups of pedestrians loitered in the open. An alleyway between two buildings was strung with ropes of laundry. The traffic on the street wasn't as thick as that of the market district, but was still busy.

Bolan approach a group of teenage boys with sullen looks on their faces. He walked up to them, smiling. He wasn't about to play the tough guy with a group of kids who could strip the Mercedes in seconds and then disappear into the urban topography like ghosts. The interest of the group perked up immediately when Bolan pulled a large number of U.S. dollars out of the pocket of his leather jacket.

Speaking in Russian, Bolan promised to match the amount of money if the Mercedes was fine when he came back from doing his business. Arrangements made, Bolan loitered long enough for the Audi to move slowly past his position on the street. He then entered the apartment building through the front door in full view of the vehicle's driver.

Bolan stepped into a stark hallway lined with the apartment doorways. A staircase to his left led to the other floors. The hall bisected the building in a straight line, and Bolan could see the rear door easily. It was held ajar by an old, stained cinder block to let in gray sunlight. Bolan turned and took up a safe vantage point just inside the door to view the Audi's actions.

In textbook manner the Audi went up the street past the mark and parked on the opposite side where the occupant of the vehicle could sit and watch his target using the rearview mirrors.

Bolan scoped out the street, figuring his approaches

from the best possible angles. He memorized the license-plate number though he had little hope that it would provide a tangible clue. Turning, Bolan moved down the hallway and out the back of the building. He moved fast, avoiding any kind of contact with the people he passed. He turned away from where the Audi was parked.

Coming out of the alley, Bolan mixed in as best he could with the flow and rhythm of the street. He crossed with a knot of pedestrians to the side of the street opposite the apartment building he had cut through, and moved past the first buildings on that block to the alley running behind them. He traversed a U-shaped pattern in an attempt to flank his shadow.

All around him the life of the republic city went on with raucous noise. Unfettered by city ordinances, the refugee inhabitants kept livestock in the form of goats, chickens, and even the occasional pig. People milled about or called down from open windows and out of doorways. Children played boisterous games and loud music from a wide mixture of cultures played and echoed down the crowded streets and alleys.

Bolan moved quickly to the mouth of the alleyway, heading for the building opposite to where the Audi was parked. He knew he'd have to move fast.

At the lip of a tiny alley Bolan halted, getting his bearings for his final approach. The Audi was parked barely twenty yards away. Bolan frowned. The engine was running. That was in the driver's favor. The Audi was not boxed in by other parked cars, but the driver's room to maneuver was severely limited. Bolan called that a draw.

Without the element of complete surprise, Bolan wouldn't have risked what he was planning.

He looked up and down the street. There were pedestrians present, but the thong of people was not immense. He did not want to risk any innocent lives and reached around behind his back and pulled out the Glock 17. He clicked his fire selector off safety. He put the hand with the pistol into the pocket of his jacket, keeping his finger on the trigger, but with the weapon safely concealed from sight.

Bolan stepped out of the alley and began walking briskly toward the car. As he'd hoped, the driver had grown lax. Instead of constantly checking his points of vision, he'd settled into surveillance mode, with his eyes fixed on his angled rearview mirror. Bolan used his free hand to remove his cell phone from his jacket pocket.

As he came even with the car, Bolan flipped his cell phone open and his thumb rapidly clicked his accessory options, bringing up the camera setting. He kicked the car door of the Audi once, holding up the phone. The driver jumped, startled, and whirled around. Bolan clicked a picture.

The driver's face went red and then white. He reached for a paper set on the passenger seat beside him. Bolan tapped the barrel of his pistol against the glass of the driver's window. At the unmistakable sound of metal on glass the driver froze. He looked up. Bolan clicked another picture. The driver was a bulky man in what Bolan estimated was his late twenties.

Slowly the man sat up.

"Roll the window down," Bolan ordered in Russian.

"Go to hell."

Bolan lowered his phone and leaned against the door. He tapped the muzzle against the glass twice.

"Roll down your window."

"Or what? You'll shoot? In the middle of a street like this?" The man's speech was concise. "No way."

"You didn't care last night when you tried to take me out."

The man's eyes narrowed slightly. "I don't know what you are talking about. I'm just here to meet my girlfriend."

"Was that your boy I got last night?" Bolan asked, goading the man. "The one who screamed and cried like a baby? You guys close?"

"I don't know what you're talking about," the man said, his voice tight with emotion.

Bolan's opinion of the man dropped. That he could get to him so easily spoke a lot less to the Executioner's interrogation skills than it did to the man's internal discipline. Bolan tired of baiting the driver. It was pointless.

It was a stalemate, and Bolan knew it. He'd taken a chance and it wasn't playing out how he wanted it. He wasn't going to blaze away with his pistol on an open street unless the guy went for his own gun. Without that as a threat, the shadow didn't feel the need to cooperate. Bolan had disrupted the survey operation and had the means to identify the agent. He would take the situation as a win.

"Get the hell out of here," Bolan said. "I know your face. If I see you again, I'll assume you're there to take me out. I don't care if it's Sunday Mass in a cathedral or Friday prayers in a mosque. I'll come at you shooting. Now go."

The young man didn't argue. He simply put the Audi into gear and drove off.

Out of a habit of thoroughness Bolan used his phone-camera to snap a shot of the vehicle and its license plate. Quickly he e-mailed the pictures to a secure host source in his cellular network. The techs knew what to do. The digital information would be threaded and sent to a site accessed from secure servers by Barbara Price or Aaron Kurtzman.

In the meantime, Bolan had some homework to do. He crossed the street and paid off the youths loitering protectively around the Mercedes. He pulled out into traffic and headed back across town toward the covert station at Meltzer's Emporium.

9

Bolan left Kubrick's keys with the receptionist. She assigned him an assistant who seemed anxious to ensure that Bolan saw as little of the building's interior as possible. He brought Bolan the station files on both the institute and Sylvia Tan. The assistant politely refused Bolan's request for the Agency files on Sable, stating that Kubrick directed access to all of those files personally and, as he was out, the assistant could not provide them. Bolan didn't push the matter. Instead he sent the assistant to get him some food and an unending pot of black coffee.

Bolan started with Sylvia Tan.

A slow smile slid across the veteran's face when he opened the file and saw the picture of the pretty Asian woman. It matched that of the woman he had seen earlier, engaged in the highly energetic tryst with the blonde in Sanders's drop-point photographs. Part of the puzzle immediately fell into place. Bolan quickly digested the contents of her file.

It was all as Kubrick had described it. Well educated, Sylvia Tan had grown up in a comfortable Taiwan household. Her own affluence had served to make her acutely conscious of the plight of the world's poor.

Meanwhile, her talent for mathematics had led to a career in the computer industry. As a young college student in the U.S., she'd joined several leftist organizations, and it was there, apparently, that KGB facilitators began taking advantage of her conscience to interest her in work as a Communist spy.

Their appeals succeeded, and Tan had worked as a stringer agent for many years. In recent months an apparent reemergence of childhood spirituality had caused a rift with some of the more secular-orientated agendas.

First Kubrick and then Sanders had kept her under observation, and it seemed Sanders had somehow managed to make contact with Sable through Tan. It was something that Kubrick had worked on for years. But then Sanders had made every attempt to remove Kubrick from the loop. If it was simply personal animosity between the two agents, then why hadn't Sanders gone to Lich?

Bolan leaned back in his chair. He drank the dregs of the coffee in his cup and put it down. He felt like a bloodhound tracker, following a trace to find the trail of his quarry. Instead of footprints and bent blades of grass, or scrapped tufts of fur, he was following conjecture, innuendo and rumor. The longer he took the colder the trail got.

He pushed away Tan's file and reached for the file on the institute itself. It was much thicker than Tan's, and the chronology went back more than a decade. Bolan sighed. He'd been given a responsibility, a duty, and he fully intended to execute his warrant. He opened up the thick package before him and began to read.

The Caucaus Data Institute both designed computers and performed computer work for highly advanced mathematical modeling. Its work included numerous defense projects. Kubrick himself had learned that the CDI was controlled by a business consortium out of Taiwan. Bolan was well-aware that the CIA controlled real-world businesses as covers, and that it was one of the better concealed facets of intelligence gathering. It also muddied the water when certain agents crossed the lines of propriety and used classified information in order to make decisions about personal stock portfolio options.

Bolan continued reading. The current head of the CDI was Dieter Vesler. Further reports showed that for the past several years Vesler had struggled with a growing narcotics addiction. Bolan leafed through copies of Grozny police and intelligence reports stating that Vesler had several times been seen in the company of big league drug traffickers.

During the height of those activities, internal security reports had filtered their way to company offices that CDI employees were complaining of propositions by mysterious recruiters. All of this in clear violation of post*glasnost* diplomatic agreements.

In early 2000, the CDI had been tasked to perform a study of marine-based aerodynamic design and radar profiles for use in Russian naval quick-insertion fast boats. The institute had executed the commission well, discovering several useful engineering techniques.

The innovations soon began appearing in Chinese surveillance watercraft used to observe Taiwan. Red flags throughout both Moscow and Washington intelligence communities had resulted in Kubrick leading an above table security project to clean up the institute. The problems seemed to have cleared up after that.

It was during that time Sylvia Tan first came under

suspicion by Grozny Station. Kubrick had made the decision to use her as a stalking horse in order to strike out at her handler, Sable. All available information pointed to Sable having gone rogue from the SVD and turned mercenary.

Bolan sat back, thinking.

How did that fit in with the information he had gained at Sanders's drop?

Sylvia Tan is a dupe. Break all contact.

Why would someone warn Sanders that Tan was a dupe? They knew she was cooperating for adversarial intelligence, so how was she a dupe? Bolan closed the file. He knew what it was time to do. It was time to go see Tan.

He strolled out of the offices without telling anyone that he was leaving, but he knew no move of his had gone unmonitored. He decided to go back to the safehouse. He was going to pay Tan a visit at her home, but she wouldn't get off work from the institute until later in the afternoon.

The woman had resisted Kubrick but had aligned herself with Sanders. Now Sanders was missing. As far as Bolan was concerned the woman was a hostile agent who had bitten the hand that fed her.

Bringing bad dogs back into line was one of the things Bolan did best.

OUTSIDE THE WINDOWS of Sylvia Tan's upscale apartment in the International District the night sounds of Grozny began to stir. Streetlights clicked on and neon signs flickered. Brothels and trendy bistros began to see an upswing in business as citizens put the day's work behind them. Traffic first thickened, punctuated by the blare of horns, and then thinned as the main arterials bled off the human excess. At various points bored Russian soldiers manned security checkpoints.

A slight breeze brought the smell of the river with it as it flowed in through Tan's open apartment windows. The aroma was pungent but muted and in the background. The air hinted rain as the sun slid down out of the sky.

Bolan set his cell phone on the table beside his chair and sat in the growing dark. The report on his photos had come back in text format while he waited. The operator had been an unknown. The Audi license plate had come back as nonexistent.

Bolan took out a Victor High Standard .22-caliber pistol and began to methodically screw a sound suppressor into place. Someone hadn't stolen an existing plate from some other vehicle in an effort to throw off research. Someone had *printed* a clean plate out of whole cloth. The ramifications of that kind of logistical support were troubling.

Bolan looked up as he heard the sound of a key turning in the lock. He lowered the pistol until the muzzle covered the doorway. He breathed out through his nose, releasing his pent-up tension as the door swung open. He could see a female outline framed against the hallway light.

From deep shadow Bolan watched, weapon ready, as the figure fumbled with the light switch inside the door. He heard an exasperated sigh after the switch was flipped several times with no effect. Earlier, Bolan had simply unscrewed all the light bulbs connected to the electrical switch.

The figure entered the room carrying an attaché case

and a purse as well as a jangle of keys. As she moved farther into the room, Bolan could make out the femininity of her form more closely. He took in the sweep of brunette hair, the angle of a cheekbone, certain before he moved, that this was Sylvia Tan.

Bolan moved in quickly to close the door. He swept behind Tan, overpowering her easily. The door closed with a bang, cutting off the source of light from the hallway. He spun the woman and put her face against the wall.

He pressed the fat muzzle of the pistol suppressor against her skull, down low where it met the spine. The feeling would be unmistakable. Tan gasped in surprise and then horror. Her bags and keys tumbled from her hands and fell to the floor.

"Move and I splatter your brains on this wall," Bolan said, using vivid language to assault his quarry's psyche. It wasn't pretty, but it was brutally effective.

"Are you armed?" he asked, his lips pressed hard up against her ear.

"No, no." The woman shuddered, and she seemed close to sobbing.

His hand roamed across her body at will, insulting her, enforcing the feeling of powerlessness as he acted. He had no feelings of revulsion at his actions. He was a mechanic fixing an engine, a surgeon excising sick flesh from healthy. She had chosen to put herself in this most precarious of situations.

Satisfied, Bolan slid his rear foot back and changed his point of balance. He replaced the end of the sound suppressor with the cruel grip of his free hand. He squeezed her neck hard enough to make her gasp. Bolan spun her off to the side, throwing her into the deep cushions of a large living room chair almost the size of a small sofa.

"Stay," he snarled.

He trained his gun on the woman and reached for the dead bolt with his free hand, never taking his eyes off Tan. He found the bolt and twisted it shut. He turned fully and regarded the frightened woman. The room was still dark and he stood in shadow. Bolan had positioned the chair where Tan sat so that a bar of light from a streetlight outside ran across her face.

She looked scared and confused, and beneath that a growing anger smoldered. She was more than pretty, Bolan decided. Her clothes were tasteful and upscale. Her allegiance to leftist ideals hadn't prevented her from enjoying the fruits of her capitalistic society.

"Nice legs," Bolan said.

Tan went pale. The compliment introduced an element of fear that was new. She had a lot of things to answer for, a lot of things to be afraid of. The compliment made the situation more insidious. She crossed her legs self-consciously under the weight of Bolan's gaze.

"On th-the hall shelf there's money," she stammered.

"Yes," Bolan replied. "And in your office there are a load of diagrams from CDI that I'm sure you're not supposed to have."

Tan pressed her lips together, holding her tongue.

"We on the same page now?" Bolan asked.

Tan nodded, her pretty features unreadable.

"Good. Now I presume you understand that if you scream I will kill you. If you fail to answer my questions quickly and honestly, then I promise you will pay the price. You are a foreign national who has betrayed my government and that of its ally. This has put the lives of my fellow soldiers in jeopardy. I give not one ounce of concern about your 'human rights' in that context."

Tan's face set into a sullen frown.

"Have I impressed upon you that my intentions are serious?" the Executioner asked.

The woman's black eyes flickered to where Bolan stood, cloaked in shadow. Bright points of hate burned in her eyes.

"What is it you want to know?" she demanded.

"How long have you been a lesbian?"

Again Bolan caught Tan off balance. Her face reddened at the unexpected question, and Bolan began having serious doubts about the level of any training Tan might have had beyond her role as carrier pigeon.

"How did—what difference does that make?"

Bolan picked up one of the photos showing Tan engaged in her acrobatic tryst with the blonde.

"Are you faking that for God and country? 'Cause, wow, good work—"

"Fuck you!" Tan snapped, enraged.

"Did you turn for Sable in order to sleep with her, or sleep with her because you turned?"

"It wasn't like that!" Tan shouted.

"Oh, so this *is* Sable." Bolan said mildly.

Realizing she'd been had, Tan drew her mouth shut into the same tight line again. Bolan's methods were as subtle as haymakers but like haymakers, when they worked, they brought the other man down.

Bolan moved slowly around until he was behind the sitting Tan. He stood where she was unable to see him, where she had no idea of his posture or intention. He waited for a moment, listening to the ragged sound of her breathing. When he spoke next his voice was a soft monotone, absent of threat or innuendo.

"I had your phone records ran before I came over, Sylvia. You spend quite a bit of your free time talking to home."

"What's your point, you son of a bitch?"

"Do your parents know, Sylvia? About your alternative lifestyle, I mean. And if they do, do you think they'd like to see the truth right under their noses in color photos?"

Tan sat stiffly, her spine ramrod straight, her body quivering with the energy of her indignation.

"You gave Sable to Sanders," Bolan demanded. "Why?"

"Because she wanted me to."

"Why?"

"I don't know."

"She didn't tell her lover?"

"She'd gone freelance since the Soviet bloc crumbled. I think she'd gone completely mercenary and didn't want to tell me."

"So you sold her out," Bolan guessed. It was imperative that he keep the questions coming in as rapid a pace as he could manage to take advantage of the momentum of her mental state.

Tan didn't answer.

"Where is she? Is Sanders with her?"

Tan didn't answer.

"Sylvia," Bolan prodded gently, "don't make me use drugs."

"She's holed up in a hotel with Sanders," Tan said.

"You've already told your control, given them a heads-up that she's gone rogue."

"No. She was my only contact. I have no way of knowing who to go to now that Sanders is with her."

"Write the address down."

Bolan watched as the quietly crying woman got pen and paper and wrote down the address. She was an untrained operative, treated with kid gloves by her handlers and stunned by Bolan's crude, brutal methods. Subjected to field interrogation, fearful for her life and future, Bolan was unsurprised that she had broken quickly. But Bolan did not trust easy. Easy got people killed.

He took the paper from her shaking hand.

"Take it," she spit.

"You want to live, Sylvia?"

The fear was naked in the woman's eyes. A hand went to her mouth. A low moan escaped her. Tan shut her eyes tightly and seemed to steel herself. She straightened and opened her eyes, staring straight into the shadowed face of the Executioner.

"Go ahead, kill me then," she said quietly.

"Nope." Bolan shook his head. "Doesn't work that way. You cooperated, Sylvia. I'll follow this lead. If it pans out, if you've told the truth, if you've not tried to warn them, then things will go well," Bolan said.

"You'll leave me alone?"

"You'll be able to go on with your life," Bolan said. "But if this falls through in any way—even if there's some freak of nature earthquake, I'll blame you and I'll come back."

"Go to the address," Tan said. "Go, you'll see."

Bolan sat across the street from the address Tan had given him. He was in a poor neighborhood on the southeast side of the city, nearing the countryside. Tan's lead was a run-down motel set in an old industrial area. Obviously built on the cheap, the place looked shabby. Made up of fifteen single-story units running from the office in an L-shape, the entire establishment looked dark and deserted. Three cars sat in the otherwise empty parking lot.

Bolan was alone, without support, working on his own terms, following his own personal rules of engagement. This was how he worked best. He could be a leader, or work flawlessly as a member of a team, but in the end, Mack Bolan was a loner. He was built that way and the forging of his personal will into a steel sword of determination had only served to accentuate those natural tendencies in himself.

Danger was something the Executioner preferred to face alone. It was his way, his chosen environment and, within the confines of that violent world, he operated at a level of excellence far beyond the norm. He saw his abilities as gifts, and he knew that having such powerful, dangerous gifts brought with them great responsibilities. Responsibility was both honor and burden. In most cases, whenever possible, Bolan preferred to bear his burdens himself.

Bolan got out of the car, sliding the Glock into the small of his back. He wasn't calling Kubrick or Lich. If Sanders had wanted them out of the loop, that was good enough for Bolan. Sanders had failed to make an important contact in the middle of a delicate operation. As far as Bolan knew, he was the man's only chance at survival—if he was still alive.

Bolan crossed the street, avoiding the sparse traffic. He could smell rain on the horizon, and the moon hung obscured by thick, low clouds. Bolan could see his own breath in the crisp, damp air. Reaching the other side of the street, the soldier turned left.

Hugging the fence line, Bolan circled toward the rear of the property. On either side of the motel, dilapidated warehouses sat empty. In the distance an overpass led deeper into the city. Behind the motel the Chechen countryside stretched out beyond the fence. Once at the rear of the property, Bolan stopped in a patch of shadow, broken hills to his back, and surveyed the run-down motel.

Just as in the front, all of the units of the motel had their window curtains tightly drawn. Away from the noises of the street, Bolan could hear radios playing and more than one television set turned up loud. He spotted no hidden sentries.

His eyes shifted to the motel office, saw no movement and he pressed forward. He cut to his right now to finish circumventing the building. Tan had told Bolan that Sanders and Sable were holed up in room 11.

Fat drops of rain began to fall on the broken pavement of the motel parking lot. Reaching unit 11 Bolan paused, head cocked to one side as he listened. He heard the sound of a television set coming from inside the target room. The noise overrode any other sounds that might have come from inside the motel unit.

Bolan looked at the door with the burnished metal, twin numeral ones set into it. The door was cheap wood, the paint was peeling and no spy hole had been bored into it. However, the window next to the door would allow the occupants to peek through the curtains and look out to see who was at the door.

Bolan was at a disadvantage. The occupants of the room would be able to identify him before he had any inkling of who was on the other side of the door. Tan had seemed genuinely cooperative, genuinely afraid. That meant nothing. Bolan thought of retreating back to the car and keeping the place under surveillance for a while.

He rejected the idea. If he had been tailed to Tan's apartment, then he could already be compromised. If time hadn't been of the essence, then the DNI would have sent someone else to ferret out what was going down here in Grozny. Sable had been sitting on a treasure trove of information, even before she had presumably gotten possession of Garabend's laptop.

Bolan made his decision to act. He stepped over to the window and rapped his knuckles against the dirty glass pane. He stepped back so that he had an equal field of vision between anyone opening the room door or pulling back the window curtain to peek out.

Bolan heard the volume on the television set in the room being turned down. A shape cast a distorted shadow across the hanging curtain. He heard a voice murmur something indistinct. A second voice, equally faint, answered. The shadow moved away from the curtain.

Bolan prepped for any possibility. Adrenaline flooded his body.

An olive-skinned, masculine hand grasped hold of the curtain hanging in the window. Time stretched out as the man drew it back. Bolan caught movement as the person inside the room shifted to peek around the curtain. A pair of black eyes met Bolan's own blue ones. Both sets of eyes widened in recognition. The Executioner snarled at the driver of the Audi and the other man released the curtain.

The Glock appeared in Bolan's fist. He stroked the trigger repeatedly, sending half a dozen rounds through the window as he skipped backward. Glass shattered under the impact of his 9 mm rounds. A burst of automatic gunfire erupted in answer from inside of the motel room.

A brilliant flame of unsuppressed muzzle-flash splashed behind the curtain. Bullets ripped through the air around Bolan and sailed out across the parking lot. The Executioner went to one knee and fired a tight trio of bullets into the curtain. He heard shouting as his rounds found a target, and then the curtain was ripped aside as a body crashed through and rebounded off the windowsill.

Bolan shifted to the left, putting himself at an angle to both the window and the door. From his vantage he had a good view of a large segment of the room. Figures moved inside the confines, and he hurriedly searched for some sort of cover.

There was nothing. There was no cover for him to get behind, nor any he could outrace a fusillade of bullets to reach. He was caught in the open by opponents who wielded superior firepower. Two men rushed forward, Bizon-19 submachine guns up at the ready.

Bolan threw himself flat out on the pavement, brought up his Glock and sighted from the prone position. He squeezed his trigger coolly and an untidy third eye opened up on the forehead of one of the gunmen. A red mist appeared behind the man's head and he crumpled forward, his submachine gun tumbling from slack fingers. The falling man's corpse fell halfway out through the shattered window.

The second gunman flinched as his comrade's sticky, hot blood and brain matter splattered across his face. The man's triggered burst sailed wild as he jerked in surprise at the gore splatter. Bolan shifted his pistol's aim to center mass and pulled the trigger on the Glock twice.

The man staggered backward like a punch-drunk fighter, arms flailing wide. Bolan brought down the muzzle of the Glock, sighted and put a final round through the man's throat. He was driven down by the kinetic force of the 9 mm bullet.

Unsure of how many others might be in the hotel room, Bolan rushed forward. He heard shouts coming from the other rooms around him, a woman screamed, and doors were opened and then slammed shut again. He knew that within minutes, heavily armed Grozny special police units would be on their way.

The front door to the room next to the gunmen's popped open, and a shirtless man with a sagging stomach and a walrus mustache looked out. A clear glass bottle was still clenched possessively in one fat fist. Bolan twisted at the hip, centering his Glock on the man. The fat Russian's face dropped in surprise.

"Get back in the room!" Bolan shouted in Russian.

The man staggered, throwing himself backward, and slammed his door shut. Bolan shifted his attention back to room 11. The inside of the room was fully engaged in flames, and Bolan realized the fire would spread quickly. People would have to get out of their rooms immediately or face being burned alive.

The soldier began to back away from the room toward where his car sat parked across the street. Black smoke poured out through the shattered window and billowed up into the sky. Flames licked at the edges of the window, completely unaffected by the slight rainfall. Bolan turned sideways away from the room, still watching it, and began to move at a faster pace back toward his vehicle.

A gunman came through the window screaming. His Bizon-19 submachine gun fired wildly as he leaped over the sill. Bolan again threw himself flat as a wild, ragged spray of rounds slapped out in his direction. He hit the pavement hard and grunted.

Thrusting his arm out straight, Bolan rolled onto his side as he tried to target the charging man. Still firing, the man shuffled toward the nominal protection of a dented car. He went to one knee behind the bumper of the vehicle and brought his weapon to his shoulder.

Bolan didn't hesitate. He rolled onto his stomach and took his Glock in both hands. His first shot hit wide of the gas hatch. His second punctured it. A jet of gasoline shot out of the hole in an arc and splashed the ground.

Bolan squeezed his trigger twice and put two more bullets through the bleeding gas tank. The second bullet ignited the flammable gases trapped inside the tank. A ball of flame erupted out and was followed hard by a wave of concussive force.

The gunman was knocked clear of the car by the

force of the explosion. His hair ignited and he rose screaming, dropping his submachine gun and slapping at the flames licking around his head. Bolan quickly reloaded, then dropped him with a precise 9 mm slug to the head.

Bullets ricocheted off the pavement a yard to the front of where Bolan lay prone on the asphalt. He pivoted his head toward the building and saw a gunman standing in the doorway of the motel room. The man had been sighting in on Bolan when the vehicle had gone up. His burst had been knocked wide in his surprise at the sudden force of the exploding automobile. He'd cringed from the rolling heat, one arm thrown up protectively over his face.

Bolan twisted, rolling up onto his left shoulder and bringing his pistol to bear on the target. He pulled the trigger once and the man's frame shuddered. Blood spurted from a hole in the gunner's upper thigh, and he sagged against the door frame. The man swept up his weapon as Bolan sighted in again.

The Executioner fired and hit the man in his stomach, then put a second 9 mm bullet into his sternum. The man's clothes billowed out under the twin impacts and he dropped, collapsing inward on himself. Blood pumped out rapidly in a growing pool around his body. His weapon clattered against the sidewalk, skittering past the door to the motel room. His eyes fixed open.

Bolan rose. In the distance he heard the sound of sirens. He turned and sprinted for his car. He'd been set up. Anger burned inside him as hot as the flames that devoured the car and building behind him.

He ran across the street and slid behind the wheel of his car. He threw the still smoking pistol on the passenger seat beside him and pulled his car keys from his front jacket pocket. The engine roared to life.

Bolan heard the shriek of sirens and looked up in his rearview mirror. Red lights spun on the top of the compact police car that was arriving first on the chaotic scene. Slower moving, but more heavily armored, troop carriers would be following behind the lead cars. If the first officer on the scene decided the situation warranted it, Sikorsky gunships could be mobilized almost immediately from military bases around Grozny.

Bolan tensed, then relaxed as the car shot past him and turned into the parking lot of the now fully engulfed motel structure. Bolan stepped on the accelerator and turned his vehicle in a tight semicircle. Straightening, he smoothly powered his car down the street. He checked his mirror. An overweight woman in a loud housedress had run from the motel office. She rushed up to the police car and began frantically pointing in Bolan's direction.

The soldier pushed the accelerator to the floor. He had to make his escape before the police got a good look at his vehicle or its license plate. Once he had procured the motel's address from Tan, Bolan had taken city maps and planned both his approach and a successive series of escape routes depending on likely variables. He hadn't had time to drive any of the routes, but he had worked to memorize them. Under pursuit now, Bolan immediately launched into one of his preset blueprints for evasive action.

He locked up his rear wheels and spun the car in another tight circle, keeping his transmission in a lower gear. Straightening, Bolan punched the gas and shot down a narrow secondary street. Two city blocks down he repeated the maneuver, shooting into a service alley. His speed was dangerously high as he sought to execute his turns before the following police cruiser could spot his taillights and pursue.

His tires screamed in protest as Bolan attempted the near ninety-degree turn. As soon as the nose of his car was pointed in the right direction, he trod on the accelerator. The tires caught and Bolan speed-shifted up through two successive gears. He blasted out of the alley and onto a dark and narrow street.

Slamming the vehicle into position between other automobiles on the avenue, he gunned the car forward, ignoring the angry blasts of horns. He wove quickly in and out of the light traffic, keeping to right-hand lanes for the quick turn whenever threatened by stops or intersections.

In the rearview mirror Bolan could see a column of black smoke rising into night. The silhouette of the city's skyline was backlit by the fire. A yellow fire engine screamed past him in the other lane followed by a security vehicle filled with armed soldiers. On the street, pedestrians emerged from bars and apartment buildings to stare and gossip.

Bolan arranged his features into a grim mask and drove deeper into the city.

Bolan entered Sylvia Tan's apartment building.

He carried his silenced Victor .22 out and ready, held down by his leg. Enough time had passed that, by now, Tan had to know her trap had backfired. Bolan had circled the building before entering and had encountered no surveillance teams on the street.

The lights of Tan's apartment were off, as was the whole of her apartment building. Televisions and stereos had all been shut off as the inhabitants of the building put their children to bed and retired themselves.

Bolan mounted the stairs leading to Tan's apartment. If she was smart, she'd already fled, Bolan figured. In which case he needed to make a careful search of her residence before moving on to follow down other leads. If, for some reason, the woman had failed to flee, then Bolan would be forced to take up the trail where he had left off.

Reaching the second floor, Bolan stopped at the corner of a wall and reconnoitered the dark hallway. It was empty and silent, with soft overhead fixtures providing a subdued illumination. Bolan looked toward Tan's doorway where a bar of dark space separated the edge of the door from the jamb.

Bolan scowled to himself. There was no good reason for Sylvia Tan's front door to be standing open at one o'clock in the morning. Had she simply run, leaving her door open? Was she there, waiting with a weapon? Had someone been sent to clean up the mess? If so, who?

Bolan started down the hallway. He held his pistol up and ready and he walked carefully, back to the wall, trailing hand out for support. He moved slowly, crossing one leg over the other. He chose to hug the inside wall because he estimated that if someone was covering the hallway from just inside the door, the person would have to shift or even open the door farther to get off an accurate shot, giving him a warning.

Moving down the hall Bolan felt naked and exposed under the overhead lights. Any resident looking out his or her peephole as he passed would see him clearly, pistol out and ready. The alternative, keeping his pistol hidden and approaching the door openly was too suicidal to even be considered at this point.

Reaching the door to Sylvia Tan's apartment, Bolan halted. He cocked his head, listening. He could hear nothing from inside the apartment through the open door. Pressing against the wall for support, Bolan carefully placed the heel of his right foot against the edge of the door.

After a long, tense moment Bolan pressed firmly with his heel, pushing it down toward the floor. The partly open door swung wide without the slightest hint of resistance and almost noiselessly on well-oiled hinges. Bolan waited for a moment, poised for action.

When no reaction was forthcoming, he carefully slid down until he was crouched beside the now fully open door. Bolan put his free hand down and pivoted smoothly around it. He leaned over to the side in a base runner's stretch, trailing leg cocked outward to help keep his center of balance, enabling him to shift in either direction quickly.

Bolan shot a brief glance around the door before pulling his head back again. He had seen nothing, no figures, no movement. Slower this time, Bolan peeked around the corner and took a longer look. He scanned the interior of the apartment. A breeze stirred the curtains of the window he had opened earlier. Other than that, he detected no motion.

The Executioner stood and quickly stepped through the doorway and into the room. He slid his back against the wall just inside the door, under the light switch Sylvia Tan had tried to use so futilely earlier that same evening. He swept his pistol around in muscle memorized patterns of movements, efficiently clearing his zones.

Finding nothing, Bolan rose and gently closed the door. He didn't turn on the lights—if Tan had even reconnected them—for fear of alerting any sentries set to survey the building, or on the off chance that someone was still here, hidden deeper in the living quarters. Bolan began to methodically move around the apartment, clearing each room before moving on.

He headed through the living area into the kitchen. He cleared the main bathroom and a hall closet. He moved into the guest bedroom Tan had remodeled into a small office, the office where Bolan had found the classified institute documents. That room was clear, as well. Warily, Bolan approached the final door at the end of the hall. It had been pulled shut and no light shone from underneath it.

Bolan held up his silenced pistol. The bulky cylinder of the sound suppressor rested even with the rise of his cheekbone. The pad of his finger tip rested confidently on the trigger of the weapon, taking up any slack in the pull. The weapon was close enough that he smelled the mellow scent of the oil he had used to lubricate the pistol.

At such close range the hollowpoint ammunition would more than compensate for the light powder charge and small caliber. Bolan had used it to devastating effect in the past. He reached out and grabbed hold of the handle to Sylvia Tan's master bedroom. He flexed his grip and slowly twisted it open.

The door swung easily under his hand, revealing a bedroom cloaked in darkness. Bolan paused in the hall, listening, and then entered the room, his pistol tracking. He moved past a dresser and then the large bed. The drawers to the dresser were open, and articles of clothing hung haphazardly from them. The covers on the bed were thrown back and a pillow lay forgotten on the floor.

Bolan crept deeper into the room. He checked an open closet, saw only coats and sweaters. He closed the closet door and went forward. His shoes made no sound on the thick bedroom carpet. The loudest noise in the place was the sound of his own breathing. He crossed the bedroom and reached the door to Tan's en suite bathroom.

Bolan turned the handle and pushed the door wide. The open curtains of the bathroom window let the soft illumination from the street into the little room. He saw the figure immediately and dropped his pistol to cover it. Sylvia Tan stared up at him.

In the ambient light her eyes were open and glazed

with the film of death. Her jaw hung slack and her skin glowed softly, like the alabaster of a statue. Bolan's gaze traveled down from her face and took in her neck. The nylon cord wrapped there bit cruelly into her throat, and the flesh had swollen up and pushed over the rope where her bodyweight pressed hard up against it.

The cord was looped around her neck and tied to the crank handle of the open bathroom window. Her arms hung loose by her side, and her knees were splayed open. Only the nylon cord kept her perched upright on the toilet.

She wore no more than a flimsy negligee, almost see-through, and clearly intended for a lover's eyes and not lounging around the house on some lazy Sunday morning. Her hair hung loose in silken tresses.

Did she deserve to die in such a manner?

The woman had been a traitor. Whether for ideals or for money, or even for love, Bolan couldn't say. But Sylvia Tan had betrayed her trusts.

End of story.

Bolan squatted, sliding his pistol into the inside pocket of his leather jacket. He ran his eyes over every square inch of the woman that he could make out in the uncertain light. Was this act a suicide or had someone silenced a liability? The question was vital and its answer imperative.

Bolan saw no evidence of bruising anywhere but around the dead woman's neck. He carefully checked between her fingers, the crooks of her arms and the bend of her knees. He was looking for hypodermic puncture marks in the hidden recesses of her anatomy. He found none. But then again, he was searching in poor lighting.

Bolan searched carefully through her hairline. Again, he found nothing, though that might simply mean he hadn't discovered what he was looking for and not that it wasn't there to begin with. He picked up and looked over her hands. A nail had broken off on the right pinkie finger. He looked on the floor of the bathroom but didn't see the piece of broken fingernail.

The soldier tore off a piece of toilet paper from the roll set in the counter next to Tan. He folded it into quarters, carefully pressing creases into the paper. Satisfied, Bolan pulled out his knife and opened it with one hand.

He rested on one knee and propped Tan's hand on his other. Using the tip of the knife, Bolan carefully scraped the residue from underneath her manicured nails and into the creases he had formed in the toilet paper. He repeated the process with her other hand.

He set the knife down, letting the limp hand fall away. He refolded the tissue and then folded it over again. Bolan slipped the tight little packet into the pocket of his jacket before picking up the knife and slipping it away.

He could smell the lingering scent of Sylvia Tan's perfume. In the distance he abruptly heard the wail of approaching police sirens. There were no coincidences in Bolan's world. The police had been alerted to the apartment.

He felt certain the Russian police units were coming for him.

Bolan moved quickly through the apartment. If time had permitted, he would have tossed the place out of careful habit, but he was satisfied it had already been sterilized by whomever Sylvia Tan had broken her fingernail struggling against. Sterilized by whoever had strangled her to death and then put her naked body in the pose of a suicide.

Bolan broke into a jog and, leaving the back hallway, he cut through Tan's living room and headed for the front door to her apartment. He was parked several blocks away to make his approach more unobtrusive. The last thing he wanted was a confrontation with Grozny military police units.

He reached up to unsnap the dead bolt to the apartment door. Outside in the street the wailing police siren became deafening as a patrol car screeched to a halt outside. The light bar revolving on the top of the vehicle cast wild patterns through the curtains in alternating flashes of light and dark illumination.

Bolan threw open the door and hurried out into the hallway. He raced to the back stairwell, since the first police car was arriving at the front of the building. Bolan plunged down them, moving fast. His footsteps were loud in the narrow passage as he quick timed down the stairs.

Reaching the bottom, Bolan threw open the door, stepped through it and stopped dead. The back stairs led out onto the entrance hall of the apartment. The back door to the building was almost immediately on his right, but in full view of the front doors. He turned and began crossing the short stretch of space between the stairs and the back entrance to the apartment building.

He heard the front door to the apartment building fly open and heard angry shouts in Russian commanding him to stop. As he ran, he risked a look back over his shoulder and saw two gray-uniformed special police unit officers, weapons already drawn.

Without thinking of the consequences, Bolan simply hurtled himself through the door and outside.

The gunfire boomed loud in the sound tunnel of a hallway and bullets cracked into the wood of the door as Bolan leaped out. He spotted a fence across a tiny square of lawn and made for it.

Images were coming at him like flashes in a viewfinder, incongruous and overwhelmingly rapid. Bolan's awareness swelled with each burst of adrenaline. He ran toward the fence, avoiding random obstacles in the courtyard that threatened to bring him down: trash cans, empty bottles, bits of refuse. At the same time he was keenly aware of geography and movement beyond his own line of sight.

He could hear the shouting of the police as they sprinted down the hall behind him, and Bolan caught the flashes of lights turning on inside apartments. He heard more police vehicles racing onto the scene. He moved instinctively, not bothering to identify each threat before avoiding it, like a running back breaking free from the line of scrimmage.

This night was turning into a real hell ride, Bolan thought as he threw himself into the air. He caught the top of the fence and heaved himself up and over. His belly scraped painfully over the rough wood of the high fence. He kept one hand in a solid grip on the top of the fence and slapped the other one down at arm's length so that he could push away from the fence as he fell.

Swinging his legs over, he somersaulted onto the ground, landing on both feet, dropping at the knees to absorb the shock. He pivoted first left and then right. Bolan was in an alley between the lines of apartment buildings. It was wide and relatively clean but not particularly well lit. One end of the alley let out to his right and was closest to the direction where he had parked his car.

Bolan dug his heels into the ground, exploding into a sprint like a racer out of the blocks. His hands cut in perfect time to his steps, increasing his speed. He sucked in energy-giving oxygen and expelled it forcefully. His legs drove down into the ground and propelled him forward.

Time stretched for him, reaching out from the center of his perception. Out of the wailing chorus of sirens, one suddenly spiked loudly above the others. A revolving pattern of light abruptly materialized, casting wild shadows on the alley walls. Bolan heard the squealing of locking brakes, tires screaming in protest. The police car shot into the mouth of the alley, directly into Bolan's path. Headlights pinned him in midstride.

Bolan didn't think, he simply reacted, moving automatically and trusting his instincts. He spun sideways and threw himself nearly prone into the direction he had just come from. He dug in and erupted back down the alley. As he ran Bolan heard car doors thrown open and the chatter of keyed-up Russian police troopers.

Ahead of him Bolan saw the first of the troopers from Tan's building clear the fence and land on the other side. The man popped out of his crouch and reached for the gun he'd holstered while scaling the fence. His eyes went wide as he saw Bolan hurtling toward him.

The Executioner raced in close, leaping into the air at the last moment as the police officer abandoned his gun and attempted to fall back into a defensive martial-arts stance. Bolan drove his knee straight into the man's side, knocking the wind from his lungs and throwing the smaller man back against the fence.

The police officer stumbled back and Bolan moved in, as relentless as a jackhammer. He clasped the shorter man with both his hands around the back of his head, using his body weight to push the man's face down. Like trip-hammers, Bolan's knees fired up, cracking hard into the line of the man's jaw near the point of his chin.

It was finished in three moves and Bolan dropped the unconscious police officer, leaving him in a heap on the ground. Not missing a beat, Bolan reached up and caught the second Russian officer as the man rolled over the top of the fence to back up his partner. Bolan hurled him to the unforgiving pavement. The man gasped for air and moaned before the soldier's foot pummeled him into darkness.

Bolan ran for it. A shot rang out, but the shooter was running as he fired and the round flew wide. Not wanting to sacrifice raw speed, Bolan made no attempt to cut back and forth as he sprinted. He simply put his head down and charged forward. Reaching the end of the alley he turned sharply to the left, putting a wall between him and the police troopers gunning for him.

Behind him more shots rang out and a distant, disassociated part of Bolan registered the angry whine of pistol rounds as they cut through the air. Windows in a car parked across the street from the open mouth of the alley shattered abruptly, scattering glass onto the street.

Out on the avenue Bolan cut to his right and sprinted across the street. He ducked between two buildings and immediately scaled a second fence. Cutting across the little courtyard, he skirted the edge of the building in the narrow space between the fence wall and the side of the structure.

Burst out onto another street, Bolan crossed it at a dead run. A red sedan locked its brakes as he cut across its trajectory. Without breaking stride Bolan leaped up and slid across the hood of the vehicle. The driver, a middle-aged woman wearing a scarf over her hair, screamed and threw her hands up to cover her face.

Bolan hit the ground on the other side of the vehicle and finished sprinting across the street. The woman slammed her hand down on her horn in outrage. Bolan pulled his keys out of his pocket as he ran, hit the electronic key fob and unlocked his car. Reaching the vehicle, he opened the door and slid behind the wheel, chest heaving.

He started the vehicle, turned around to look out his rear window, hammered the car into reverse and stomped on the accelerator.

The car responded smoothly and Bolan shot out into the street and roared past the stalled sedan in reverse, so close to it he almost sideswiped the woman's car. Once the front of his car had cleared the trunk of the sedan, Bolan turned in a tight bootlegger maneuver around the vehicle.

Pointed in the direction he'd reversed in, Bolan again worked his clutch and put the car into gear. The tires gripped the pavement and the vehicle surged forward.

Within seconds Bolan had disappeared into the labyrinth of narrow Grozny streets.

12

The Executioner put the folded paper into a plain envelope and, after getting instructions on his scrambled line, left the package in a dead drop in a men's room at the Grozny airport. Support had promised him a five-hour turnover on the bio-forensics. In the meantime, Bolan returned to the safehouse.

Sylvia Tan had led him into a trap to protect Sable. Or to keep him from Sable. If she had truly swung and was working with Sanders, then she surely would have been more forthcoming. That meant Tan, as Bolan had suspected after first seeing the photos of the two women together, hadn't turned. She hadn't turned Sable onto Sanders; she'd turned Sanders onto Sable. She'd remained loyal to her original handler.

Tan is a dupe.

That note was significant. The stringer wasn't necessarily warning Sanders about something he didn't know, but about something Tan didn't know. If Tan was still loyal to Sable, but was a dupe, that meant her control wasn't who she thought it was. She could have asked Bolan to take her in. Instead she'd been killed, silenced after setting him up.

Obviously the motel had been a field operations center. The shooters in that room were stationed there. The place had not been chosen specifically as an ambush to cross him. Otherwise he'd never have made it away alive. They'd have taken him down as soon as he'd gotten out of his car. Who needed a hit team staged in a Grozny slum, ready to roll at a moment's notice?

The list of possibilities was too extensive: international jihadists, arms dealers, drug smugglers, enforcement for Russian syndicates, affiliates of intelligence concerns, mercenaries specializing in leftist causes. The list went on.

Bolan needed another thread to run down, another way to try to locate Sanders, to find Sable. He was tired of being outgunned. The city had turned deadly on him and instead of rolling with full battlefield gear, he'd been shooting it out with a handgun. That had to change.

While making the call to arrange the blind drop, Bolan also asked for contingency equipment. There was nothing illegal in the safehouse. If it was investigated or raided by local authorities, it needed to turn up clean so as not to cast suspicion on the front company the Agency used to conduct business here. The voice on the other end of the scrambled line had assured Bolan that he would be receiving a key to a locker with just the sort of "foul weather" insurance he was looking for.

Who was left who might have a line on Sable? Bolan wondered. Kubrick claimed to be in the dark. Lich was more of a mystery than Kubrick. Who else had been up on Sable?

He forced his racing mind to slow. Baby steps. He needed to proceed with baby steps. The answers were there; he just needed perspective.

What did he know? He knew Sanders had called

from an unsecured line. Bolan stopped himself. That wasn't the beginning. Sanders had wanted to bring in Sable. He'd learned of Sable through Tan. He'd found Tan from Kubrick. Kubrick had found Tan because he'd been surveying the CDI. He'd been surveying CDI because classified material had been getting out.

He frowned. What had been getting out? He ran down the list of breaches he had seen while going over the files in the Grozny station: technology, research, financial transaction records...

Bolan began pacing. Financial transactions? Tan was a research scientist, so she probably had no more access to financial transactions than the company janitor. Someone else had given those out. Kubrick hadn't been running just Tan, couldn't have been. Who else?

Dieter Vesler, the president of CDI.

That was the only other name of note in the institute files—Vesler, who Agency records showed was sporting a serious cocaine habit and a penchant for living beyond even his generous means. Kubrick had been onto Vesler. He'd fed Tan to Sanders, but Kubrick had kept Vesler all for himself. The chance that there were two opposition control officers running doubles in the CDI were remote. If Sable was running Tan, then she was probably running Vesler.

Why this hadn't been reflected in the files troubled Bolan. Who was hiding the information, who was protecting Vesler? Kubrick? Lich? Both? Bolan looked at his wristwatch, noted the time. He got ready to go. He'd left his car, which was potentially compromised, in a multistory parking garage.

Police agencies would be looking for him, but no pictures had turned up on the news. He was wanted, but he was still anonymous. The clock was ticking rapidly and people's lives hung in the balance.

Bolan's sat phone buzzed from where it rested on the kitchen countertop. He looked at the number in the display and grunted in recognition. Things were about to start rolling. He picked up the phone.

"Go."

"Hello, Striker," Barbara Price said over the secured line.

Bolan found himself smiling, despite himself. It was good to hear the woman's voice, even if it was coming from halfway across the world.

He listened carefully to the terse but vaguely worded instructions Price gave him. He contemplated the implications of what he was hearing.

"Right. Good. Thanks, Barb," he said and hung up.

Bolan walked out of the kitchen to the front of the house. He looked out the window from behind a heavy curtain, surveying the street in all directions and elevations. Other than an old woman walking up the street carrying a small bag of groceries and a teenage boy walking a dog, the street was empty.

Satisfied, Bolan looked down to the end of the street to where his new car sat, waiting. The BMW was sleek and black, but most importantly, it had a V8 engine and would be a standard transmission as he had specified.

Bolan gathered what he needed and left the safehouse, heading down the street, alert for anything out of the ordinary. Reaching the car, he slid into the driver's seat. The interior of the automobile was antiseptically clean. He adjusted the seat and mirrors before reaching under the driver's seat and removing the keys. The German-made engine started smoothly when he turned the ignition.

Bolan opened up the glove compartment. Inside was an owners' manual and a manila envelope. Bolan pulled the envelope out and opened it. Inside was a folded piece of paper. He scanned what it read and snorted with derision. The operation in Grozny had just taken a very interesting turn.

The DNA found under Sylvia Tan's fingers belonged to Herman Kubrick.

IN THE TRUNK of the BMW, in a false bottom under the spare tire, the Agency had put the field kit Bolan had requested. As a result he wore a new bulletproof vest under his shirt and in addition to the weapons he had acquired, Bolan carried a mini-Uzi machine pistol. The Uzi combined two main factors vital in urban-based close-quarter battle. It was very easy to conceal and it put out a tremendous rate of fire.

Bolan knew he faced a very real potential of coming up against heavier ordnance, but he needed move around the city with as low a profile as he could muster. The machine pistol was a compromise in that sense. In addition, the mini-Uzi had come with an attaché case apparatus so that it could be fired by depressing a button trigger in the handle, as well as openly.

After driving for twenty minutes, Bolan pulled over to the side of the road. He lifted a pair of binoculars to his eyes and adjusted the focus on them until the house, set some hundred yards away, came into sharp focus.

Bolan concentrated his focus into tight parameters, forcing himself to become methodical, almost machine-like in his thoroughness.

He began to slowly sweep the binoculars over Kubrick's property.

The Executioner didn't project images or intentions onto his target area, but rather scanned in a completely passive mode. Sometimes the mind didn't comprehend what the eye truly saw, and only a relaxed attention could decipher the myriad of tiny clues and then put them together.

Kubrick's house was outside of the international zone reserved for dignitaries, diplomats or any foreigner working on behalf of a sponsoring government. He lived "on the economy" as it was termed in official circles. His house was in the section of Grozny where a larger Middle Eastern population contained a much smaller Asian one.

Kubrick's house was two stories set in a half-acre plot on a street lined with expensive, but tasteful homes. A ten-foot-mortar-and-charcoal-colored-stucco wall surrounded the property with a pedestrian entrance in the center of the wall, facing the street, and a double car garage set to the southeastern corner of the property.

A path wound through the property about twenty yards from both the garage and the front gate, through a small garden to the front of the house. The upper story of Kubrick's house was half open deck and half living structure with a pagoda-style roof. A red cedar deck encircled the house.

If Kubrick had domestics, or a mistress, they were not present. Thorny rose bushes had been planted underneath his windows, a crude but effective defensive system in and of itself. The front door was heavy and reinforced with hinges of iron plating, ostensibly as decoration. That art decor touch made the door nearly impenetrable to manual battering rams. If it was locked it would take an Urban Assault Vehicle or shaped charges to breach it.

Bolan frowned as he scanned the exterior of the house. From the way the sunlight glinted in reflection off the windows he could tell they were abnormally thick and more than likely designed never to be opened. An environmental control unit hummed on the roof, encased in a housing structure and padlocked.

Bolan could detect no hint of a security system, though he knew it had to be there. It was all internally based, more than likely boasting a separate generator in case of power failure.

Bolan weighed the probabilities and known facts. The government did not supply security systems as a matter of course to governmental agents living on the economy at either home or abroad. It was not conducive to operational security to have even high-level agents taking classified documents out of the minifortresses of modern intelligence buildings and into their homes. If Kubrick was crooked, however, then that was exactly what he would be doing. In all probability, then, the security system Kubrick used would be a commercial model.

Bolan swept the glasses upward, following the telephone lines from the poles to Kubrick's house. Despite the insurrection, Grozny was a modern city and an economic lynchpin in Russian-Asian finance due to its oil reserves.

No matter what model of security system—audible, infrared motion detection, pressure pads, egress contact switches, ultrasonic transceivers, glass break sensors, or even transmitters on wireless systems—they all transferred the breach alerts through the phone line.

Bolan readied himself for the next step in the process. He put the binoculars under his seat and opened the console between the driver and passenger seats. From inside he fished out a pair of latex medical gloves and pulled them on.

Bolan popped the trunk release and got out of his car. He took in the activity on the residential street as he walked around behind the vehicle. Pushing up the lid of the trunk, he reached inside, moved the contents to the side and opened a key-coded compartment set into the bottom of the trunk.

He pulled out a small leather knapsack and threw one shoulder strap over his left arm. Closing the trunk lid, he started down the street toward Kubrick's house.

It was one of the lesser-known facts of surreptitious entry that most break and enter burglaries occurred during daylight hours. It made simple, direct sense. Most people were at work during the day. Also, though it was easier to spot someone during daylight hours, they tended to raise less suspicion simply because it was daytime.

Bolan walked down the street, head up. He detected no camera presence on Kubrick's property. Reaching the garage-side corner of the wall, Bolan stepped easily off the street and into the lee of the structure. He dropped the knapsack and opened it, taking out a collapsible, tactical ladder, which he shook open. In under five seconds he had unfolded a six-foot ladder and he propped it against the wall. He looked around and tossed his knapsack over the wall.

Without hesitating, Bolan scrambled up the ladder and slid belly down on the top of the wall. He picked up the lightweight ladder and slid it onto the other side of the wall where he then scrambled down. Hitting the ground, Bolan didn't wait to see if he had been compromised breaching the wall. He sprinted forward to the side of the house, freeing a pair of wire cutters.

He went down on one knee beside the telephone box and snipped the wire in a single, efficient motion. Bolan pivoted, still on one knee, and took his initial survey. He looked back and forth across the interior of the compound, cutting it into zones, looking for motion, listening for outcries. Slowly, Bolan rose. The house and the surrounding neighborhood remained silent.

Bolan walked over to his ladder and compressed it quickly, replacing it in the knapsack and starting for the side door to Kubrick's house. Even with the phone line cut, Bolan had no intention of using the main entry point to any building.

He came up to the side door and looked in. He saw a modern kitchen, immaculately clean and filled with expensive appliances. Pulling a lock pick gun from his bag, Bolan quickly worked at the dead bolt and the main door lock set into the knob.

He eased the door open and stepped into the kitchen. He ran his eyes along the door frame and saw the magnetic connector switch alarm apparatus recessed into the door. It was a commercial system.

Bolan closed the door to the kitchen behind him softly and entered Kubrick's house. The decor theme was Asian, even Buddhist, blended with an obvious penchant for technology. Looking for an office or master bedroom, and fearing that time was tight, Bolan cut down hallways, crossed rooms, checked behind doors.

Bolan found Kubrick's home office. It was of a masculine design, boasting a huge desk, conference phones, personal computer and a globe made out of semiprecious stones. Bolan ignored the computer. In the field it was too dangerous to attempt to access files from a protected PC.

Any attempts to insert hacking software into the CPU could cause a multitude of protection programs to destroy internal software. A laboratory setting was the only risk acceptable method with an operator of Kubrick's ability, and Bolan wasn't prepared to isolate, power down and then physically remove the CPU.

He began shaking the room down, careless of making a mess. He had no intention of trying to keep the entry hidden from Kubrick. It would be nearly impossible anyway, and time was the biggest factor at that point. Bolan pulled tables out, moved paintings, pulled up carpet edges. Finally, behind a row of books, Bolan found the safe.

He swept the books aside, knocking them to the floor. Without taking his eyes off the safe Bolan shrugged his black knapsack free and opened it. The safe had a keypad access instead of tumbler. Bolan removed several items from the knapsack and placed them on the shelf like a surgical tech laying out tools for a physician.

First, he put down a small, unmarked aerosol can, then a pair of night-vision goggles followed by a small screwdriver, a cable attached to a compact black box, and finally a BlackBerry device.

Bolan keyed up the program and then set the personal digital assistant back on the shelf. Picking up the aerosol canister, Bolan triggered it and lightly misted the safe's keypad. He slipped the goggles into place and turned them on.

The aerosol spray contained a bonding solution that caused it to adhere to human skin oils. Once bonded, enzymes in the spray interacted chemically with compounds in the oils and showed up on ultraviolet spectrums. Bolan shifted the goggles from infrared to ultraviolet vision mode.

On the keypad the cluster of numbers showing fingerprints stood out in vivid relief. Bolan entered the grouping of numbers into the BlackBerry. He hit the button to activate the number crunching program and pulled his goggles off. He put his equipment away while the program calculated all the number combinations possible from the digits he'd inputted into its memory.

Bolan slid the edge of his screwdriver into the seam where the case housing for the keypad was recessed into the front of the safe. He dug in and snapped the screwdriver down, popping the faceplate. He picked up the black plastic box frame and slid it into place over the now exposed keypad.

He checked the BlackBerry and saw that it had finished running the probability calculation program. Taking the loose end of the cable, Bolan inserted it into the BlackBerry's input jack and then hit the enter key.

The BlackBerry immediately began running sequences of numbers and transmitting them to the Field Electronic Interdiction and Disruption Device. The FEIDD began to manipulate the keypad faster than a human could, clearing the instrument after each usage so that a total Sequential Access Attempt record failsafe would not be triggered. The black plastic box hummed slightly and from inside of it Bolan heard a rapid clicking of keys, like a court reporter working a stenograph.

In under three minutes the BlackBerry display froze on a numeric sequence and the safe popped open as the locking mechanism was disabled. Bolan quickly broke down the BlackBerry and FEIDD, replacing them in the knapsack. He reached up and opened the safe.

It was stuffed full of items. There were several passports and ID cards under various names, all with Kubrick's picture, as well as a 9 mm Heckler & Koch VP-70M sitting on top of an accountant's ledger, and stacks of money in various currencies. In the back there was single black video cassette devoid of markings. All of these items were stacked on top of a business-size manila envelope sealed with security clearance tape.

Bolan reached in and pulled out the thick envelope. He opened the package and poured out the contents. Looking quickly through the mess, he searched for names or locations that could give him some hint to the Sable situation. From the clearance codes stamped across the files and documents, it was obvious that Kubrick was bringing home a lot more from work than he should have.

As Bolan scanned the papers, two important points jumped out at him. Kubrick was in deep, and he was an arrogant son of a bitch. Excerpts and titles flashed out at Bolan like light bulbs exploding in his face. It was all right there like a recipe or a grocery list. Cold anger burned inside of Bolan, as he scanned the documents.

One paper included a damning statement. *Have secured false-flag recruitment of Sylvia Tan. She believes herself to be working for Sable's superior and control.*

Bolan rifled through the pages. He came across a list of more than a dozen names and a timetable showing the efforts of several of those names in taking out Sanders and Sable. Most of the operational plans centered on either the casino or the porn theater.

The operations center for the group was listed as the

Grozny motel where Sylvia Tan had sent Bolan. At the bottom, hastily scribbled in a bold hand, was an annotation. *Since these attempts, subjects have not used drops or made covert office contact. We must believe they suspect.*

The last document in the bundle was a list of opposition agents in Grozny. On the list was Peter Sanders and a woman named Katrina Alexi. Bolan deduced that had to be Sable. Sylvia Tan's name was below that with the note *"Kind Judas"* written beside it.

Kind Judas was Agency cant for an unwitting friendly agent. At the bottom of the paper another note had been scribbled in the same bold hand as before: *Unknown oppositional asset remains active at the CDI.*

Bolan began stuffing the papers into his knapsack. Kubrick had Sanders listed as opposition, but Lich hadn't passed that information on through channels. A wet work op had been initiated on Sable without Washington's approval.

Bolan knew for sure that Kubrick believed Sanders was Sable's, and that he wanted to take them out, but it didn't answer the question of precisely why. No wonder Sanders had avoided the covert station and gone to ground. Kubrick had been trying to kill him. But if he was Sable's, as Kubrick stated, then why had he tried to contact the Agency at all?

Tan had thought herself working for Kubrick against Sable by the end, true to her ideology over her own personal feelings for Sable. Even to the point of selling her out? She'd sure as hell been ready to do *him* in, Bolan thought. She'd sent him into Kubrick's viper nest at the Grozny motel without hesitation. But the shooters there hadn't been expecting his arrival. That made sense if Tan had known where the squad was based, but hadn't known how to contact them directly.

To throw Bolan off she had sent him into a dangerous situation and then called Kubrick to alert the team. Only Bolan had beat Kubrick's alert message and Kubrick had silenced Tan. But how had he beaten a phone call across a city? Perhaps the shooters had been gathered under a cover and hadn't known they were working for Kubrick.

But Tan on the other hand...Tan had known exactly how to get in touch with Herman Kubrick and exactly what he'd looked like. Once Kubrick was aware Bolan had found Tan, she'd obviously become too great of a risk for the agent. But risk to what? What was Kubrick protecting?

From behind him, at the front of the house, Bolan heard a door open and then slam shut again.

The sound of the slamming door reverberated through the house. Reaching up to his knit cap, Bolan pulled it down over his face so the balaclava obscured his features. Kubrick wasn't the kind to give his security codes out to his cleaning woman, Bolan thought. The traitor had arrived.

Bolan swung the knapsack onto his shoulders and shrugged it into position. He crossed the room toward the door, moving fast. His mind was racing as he ticked off options.

He reached out and grabbed the handle of the office door. He twisted it slowly and then, when it unlatched, lifted up slightly as he swung it open, preventing the hinges from squeaking.

The door swung open easily. Bolan straightened, shifting his body position. When it was about halfway open, the door was suddenly kicked toward him.

Bolan was knocked back by the force of the blow. He staggered, arms windmilling to catch his balance. Kubrick burst through the entryway hard on the heels of the swinging door. He charged straight into Bolan, pressing his attack. The man was big and fast for his size. He used a shuffling sidestep while throwing haymakers and pressing his advantage.

Bolan momentarily retreated, hands up defensively. Kubrick's big fists hammered through his guard, driving against his lowered face. Bolan rocked from the impact of the big punches, reeling under their force, staggering backward.

He came up against the desk and was bent backward under Kubrick's onslaught. The change of position left him vulnerable but also changed his elevation, forcing Kubrick to reorient himself to continue his attack.

Kubrick turned to face Bolan fully and thrust himself up and forward, leading with a big, right-handed, hammer blow.

The expression on Kubrick's face was oddly detached, like a man performing some slightly odious, but necessary task. It was red from his exertion but betrayed no emotion whatsoever. Shoved up this close to the man's bulk and mammoth power, Bolan realized Kubrick was heavily muscled under a misleading layer of cosmopolitan fat.

Kubrick leaned in over the awkwardly positioned Bolan and brought his right hand down toward the Executioner's exposed face. Bolan made no attempt to block the powerful blow. Instead, as the arm came down Bolan turned his head to the side and lifted his left shoulder toward the strike while wrapping his arms around the descending fist in a hugging maneuver.

Bolan winced as the strike hammered into his shoulder and neck hard enough to rattle his teeth before he snapped his trap closed. Bolan's right hand captured Kubrick's arm at the wrist while his left arm snapped up and bent back to grab the same wrist, pressing his elbow and forearm in a parallel position with Kubrick's own grasping arm.

Joint lock in place, Bolan grasped as hard as he could and twisted like a snake around Kubrick's grip. His legs came up and wrapped themselves around Kubrick's upper arm, sinking in a brutally tight lock at the bigger man's wrist and elbow. One foot pushed hard into Kubrick's face while the second foot found position under the bigger man's extended arm.

Bolan threw himself over, holding Kubrick's trapped arm tightly to his torso. The agent grunted with the sudden pain and was thrown off his feet beside the desk. Still gripping the hyperextended arm, Bolan threw himself backward off the desk. Kubrick screamed.

The sound of the elbow popping was sharp, the sound of the shoulder coming out of its socket was more muted. Both men fell to the floor, and Kubrick screamed again.

The big man was frantic to shake Bolan loose but couldn't shift his bulk quickly enough to rise. Bolan, refusing to let go of his opponent's mangled arm, began to hammer the heel of his foot into the man's face.

Kubrick's head rocked with each impact, but Bolan felt as if he were putting his boots to stone. The flesh of Kubrick's right ear tore and blood soaked the side of his face, running freely down into his mustache and beard. Bruises blossomed on Kubrick's cheek and face. The tread of Bolan's boot tore an ugly gash in the agent's forehead above his bushy eyebrows.

Kubrick swung his bulk around until he was facing Bolan. With his free hand he began shoving at the legs entangled around his injured arm. Bolan felt the big man's weight shift and rolled sharply with the changing leverage. Bolan spun with the trapped arm in the opposite direction, brutally reversing angles.

Kubrick screamed again and was driven over Bolan's

turning body. He planted his nose hard into the carpet of his own office. Now on his belly, facing away from Kubrick with the man's arm trapped beneath him, Bolan started using his heel stomp again.

His face a bloody mask, Kubrick managed to grasp Bolan's ankle and slow the force of the kicks. Blind with pain, and beaten to a mess, the big man managed to get his legs underneath him and rise. Bolan was stunned at the amount of damage Kubrick was able to absorb. The man rose to his feet, threatening to upend Bolan in the process.

Bolan quickly changed positions. He released the man's arm just as Kubrick reared up and sought to lift Bolan from the floor. The agent stumbled backward, his balance completely compromised. He slammed hard into his bookshelf and sent leatherbound volumes spilling out across the floor. Bolan leaped to his feet and started toward the other American.

Kubrick swept the heavy globe of semiprecious stones off the edge of the desk and sent it hurtling into the rushing Bolan, who twisted to avoid the projectile. Kubrick lunged toward his open safe. Bolan knocked the globe aside and leaped toward Kubrick, remembering the automatic pistol hidden in the safe.

Bolan smashed into Kubrick, driving him up against the bookcase before the other man could access the contents of the wall safe. Kubrick grunted in pain as his mauled shoulder struck the unforgiving wall.

The Executioner lifted Kubrick up and then began rocking blows toward the big man's head. Kubrick swept his good arm back, driving the elbow into his adversary's head. Bolan rocked back, staggered. Kubrick twisted sideways and used the space he had created to lash out with a side kick.

The foot strike hit Bolan on his thigh and pushed him farther back. Bolan spun, absorbing the force of the blow and reset himself. Kubrick turned back toward the safe, plunging his good hand inside the container, scrambling for the pistol.

Even as he moved Bolan knew he was too late.

Kubrick whirled, gun in hand. Loose papers, documents and money spilled out of the safe. Snarling, the big man brought up his pistol. His right arm useless, Kubrick had grabbed the weapon with his left hand. The pistol exploded as Bolan dived forward.

Bolan felt the impact like a hammer blow low in his gut, just high enough that his vest still took the bullet and stopped the round. Two more rounds spun out, missing as recoil carried Kubrick's pistol muzzle off target.

The soldier changed tactics instinctively, throwing himself backward and leaping for the protection of Kubrick's desk. Shooting with his off hand, Kubrick fired another burst of triple shots at the diving blur his opponent had become. Bolan hit the big desk and slid across it to the other side. Kubrick's bullets slapped into his study wall.

Bolan pulled the mini-Uzi machine pistol free. Unsure of Kubrick's tactics, he fired up at an angle in case Kubrick had followed him over the top of the desk. Still firing, Bolan reached up over the edge of the desk and angled the Uzi, triggering a longer blast. Finally he stood up behind the firing weapon and sprayed the room.

The door to the hall hung open and 9 mm rounds from Bolan's weapon punched into the wall outside of the office door. Bolan squinted through gun smoke toward the door. Kubrick's beefy hand came around the edge and he triggered his pistol. The Executioner ducked behind the desk again and then answered with a burst that chewed up the handcrafted door frame.

Bolan rolled out from behind the desk, coming to his feet and bringing up the mini-Uzi. In the hallway Bolan heard an empty magazine strike the floor followed by the metallic click of a round being chambered. Then he heard nothing else.

Bolan's ears still rang from the deafening gunfire in such an enclosed space. He rolled over one shoulder behind the desk and came up against the wall on the same side of the room where the door opened. This angle gave him a drop of seconds should Kubrick choose to rush the room.

Weapon up, Bolan crept to the door. He heard nothing. It was not the time for half measures. The time for covert action and subtle maneuvers was past. This was a firefight.

Bolan burst into action. He thrust the mini-Uzi around the corner and opened fire. Still firing, Bolan pivoted around the fulcrum of his weapon and threw his back up against the wall on the opposite side of the door, giving himself a narrow view of the hallway.

He saw a corner of the kitchen down the short hall and could make out a piece of the marble-topped island in the center of that room. He ducked back from the opening and dropped the spent magazine from his mini-Uzi. He slammed home a fresh one and released the bolt on the Uzi, priming the weapon for use. A haze of gun smoke hung in the air.

Bolan swept the barrel up and stepped into the hallway, keeping to a tight crouch. His finger was taut on the trigger as he moved down the hall. Three steps down from the office door more of the kitchen revealed itself. Tensed, Bolan pushed forward.

Kubrick popped up from behind the kitchen island, triggering a triburst from his H&K pistol. Bolan threw himself backward. A ragged fusillade of rounds tore down the kill zone of the residential hallway. Bolan went to a knee and triggered the mini-Uzi, answering Kubrick vicious burst for burst. The little stuttergun unleashed a torrent of rounds into the kitchen.

Sparks flew off pots and pans hanging from a rack suspended above the island, and the utensils rang like church bells. Glass shattered in the windows behind Kubrick, reducing his cabinetwork to splinters. Skid marks streaked across the marble top of the counter and bullets ricocheted wildly.

"Cooper, I know it's you, you son of a bitch!" Kubrick shouted.

He came around the side of the counter island, popping out like some oversized, malignant Jack-in-the-box and triggering double 3-round bursts under Bolan's arc of fire. The Executioner threw himself against the inner wall of the hallway to avoid the furious spray of bullets. A third burst cut the air through the hall, pinning Bolan back.

"This won't save you Kubrick!" Bolan shouted.

He slid to one knee, still intimate with the wall. He dived forward, firing a burst, taking the force of his landing on his elbows and recentering his aim as he absorbed the shock of impact.

Bolan heard the reverberation of the slam as Kubrick's door struck the wall next to it. Instantly he realized what the agent had done. Bolan crawled forward and peered quickly around the corner. He saw the side door he had used to breach Kubrick's house standing open and knew the man was making for his vehicle, or an area he could defend while attempting to contact backup.

Bolan hopped up, machine pistol at the ready. He rushed forward, chasing Kubrick. As he came into the kitchen proper, he caught a dark flash as Kubrick threw himself through the single access door into his three-car garage. Firing through a shattered window, Bolan fired a burst after the fleeing agent. More glass shattered, but his rounds were late and the garage wall absorbed the bullets.

Bolan shifted directions, sliding over the bullet-scarred top of the kitchen island. He raced into the entrance hall leading to the front door and the formal reception area of the house.

Bolan held his weapon one-handed as he snapped back the dead bolt on the front entrance and then tore the door open. He went through the doorway fast, his Uzi up, held one-handed in close by his hip so that wherever he turned, the muzzle was perfectly aligned. He sprinted across the layered patio and thundered down the steps, securing the weapon in a two-handed grip.

Bolan heard the unmistakable rattle and hum of an electric garage door rolling up and open. Over that he heard the sound of an engine roar, revving hard as Kubrick shoved it into gear. There was the scream of peeling rubber as the agent gunned his black Mercedes into Reverse.

The Executioner crossed the garden area in the front of Kubrick's house at a dead run. He could see the street through the bars of Kubrick's pedestrian entrance. He heard the tires of the Mercedes bite into pavement and the dip in the engine's rumble as the agent transitioned from Reverse to Drive.

Rebel Force 119

Again there was a screech as Kubrick pushed the accelerator to the floor and gunned the vehicle. Bolan threw himself hard into the locked gate, thrusting the mini-Uzi through the decorative, wrought-iron bars of the gate. As sleek as a spaceship, the Mercedes with its tinted windows darted past.

Bolan didn't hesitate as he opened up with the mini-Uzi. He knew from driving the vehicle earlier that it had bullet-resistant glass and reinforced bodywork, but he refused to make even one second of Kubrick's escape easy. The stuttergun erupted in his hand as the car shot forward, spent shell casings flying from the bucking machine pistol.

Dimples appeared on the side of the vehicle and ricocheting bullets shot sparks in the air. Bolan walked his line of fire along Kubrick's car, which continued to gain speed as it raced past Bolan. He stubbornly held down his trigger.

His rounds hammered mercilessly into Kubrick's Mercedes, knocking the hubcap on the rear wheel spinning into the street of the quiet residential neighborhood. The agent sped away and then cut the big car into a power slide as he turned hard at the first corner.

Bolan felt the vibration of his weapon cease and the sound of gunfire died as the bolt snapped back into the locked position. The soldier looped the empty Uzi from a strap around his shoulder and pulled his Glock out from behind his back. He pulled the trigger twice and shattered the lock on the gate, then lifted a big foot and slammed the gate open. Pistol up, Bolan sprinted into the street. He saw the red brake lights on the black Mercedes flash as Kubrick made the corner at the end of the street, and then Bolan heard only the sound of the powerful engine as Kubrick raced to safety.

Kubrick was on the run and knew Bolan knew he was rogue, but this revelation still hadn't saved Sanders. After almost two decades in the region, Kubrick could disappear if he chose, and Bolan knew that. That still left an American agent unaccounted for and a dangerous freelance operative on the loose.

Bolan had a single lead left after the debacle that had just occurred, and he was afraid it was a lead Kubrick might already be on to. If Kubrick caught up with the man running the Caucasus Data Institute before Bolan did, then he could ensure that his investment in Sable, whatever that might be, was safe.

In the distance Bolan heard the all too familiar sound of Grozny police unit sirens as he reached his car. He jerked open the door and threw both weapons onto the passenger seat as he slid behind the wheel. He started the vehicle and left a stretch of rubber to rival Kubrick's as he shot out of his parking spot and into the street.

Bolan whipped around a battered black Russian sport wagon stopped dead in the middle of the street. The young man behind the wheel had both his hands raised in horror to his mouth, and his eyes were big as tea saucers as Bolan gunned his vehicle past him after the fleeing Kubrick.

Every second counted. Bolan knew where Vesler was, but Kubrick knew Grozny like the back of his hand after all this time. It was *his* town. Grimly, Bolan shifted up from first gear until he had the vehicle moving flat out. He had no intention of making things easy for Kubrick, and Bolan promised himself the rogue agent was going to have to earn whatever he wanted, inch by bloody inch.

14

Bolan raced his automobile, driving it hard as he chased Kubrick through the streets. He was thrown against the restraints of his seat belt as he took his corners sharp and floored the gas through the straight stretches. He darted in and out of slower traffic as if the other vehicles were traffic cones on an engineering track. Horns blared in his wake, and his tires wailed in protest as he leapfrogged through the growing traffic.

Keeping his gaze glued to the road, Bolan reached down and rooted briefly in the open top of the knapsack he had carried into Kubrick's residence. He secured his extra magazines for the mini-Uzi and tossed them onto the passenger seat. He maneuvered around a construction truck and then squeezed in between two passenger vehicles and a bus. Bolan picked up the mini-Uzi and hit the clip release, ejecting the spent magazine.

He tucked the still warm barrel of the weapon between his legs and inserted a fresh 30-round magazine into the well of the buttstock. He picked up the weapon and jammed the bolt handle up against the underside of the dash and shoved sharply, cocking the weapon one-handed.

Bolan jerked his car back into line, saw Kubrick

ahead of him and gunned his car forward. He knew Kubrick had to be on his phone by now, alerting Lich to the situation, perhaps calling in reinforcements. If Bolan was going to get to Sable first, then he had to beat Kubrick to Vesler.

The time it took for reinforcements to arrive was time Kubrick could use to get to the head of the Caucasus Data Institute and find Sable. Like a bloodhound on the scent, Bolan had followed the trail of clues and blood across the length of the city.

As was always the case, the closer he got to the lair of the monster, the more dangerous the quest became. The trail Bolan had picked up in Grozny would go as cold as Sable's corpse if Kubrick wasn't stopped.

Bolan gained on the fleeing Kubrick by increments of feet at every turn and at every ebb and flow of traffic that forced the racing vehicles to alter their speeds. Each time the quickness of response that Bolan's standard transmission held over Kubrick's automatic was enough for him to methodically close the distance with the rogue agent.

Bolan was racing not only against Kubrick, but also against the arrival of Russian authorities. So far there were only angry drivers and panicked pedestrians to witness their reckless cat-and-mouse chase, but the stakes had grown serious enough that, when he pulled close enough, a gun battle might open up.

They hit a red light and Kubrick ran it without hesitation. Bolan sped around the intervening vehicles and shot into the street. He laid on his horn and burst out into traffic. Cars racing from either side locked up their brakes and slid sideways as Bolan shot the eye of the needle. A battered old pickup swerved around a stalled sedan and tried to apply its brakes too late when the driver realized Bolan was speeding past in front of him.

The nose of the braking truck struck Bolan's car in the rear fender. The concussion jarred the solider hard, and his rear end swerved out of control. The vehicle's fender crumpled from the abrupt impact, causing the trunk to warp.

Bolan turned his wheel away from the skid his rear end was taking, trying to prevent the vehicle from spinning completely under the impact. The front-wheel drive caught, and the powerful engine churned as Bolan shifted into a lower gear. The tires gripped the pavement, and Bolan felt the vehicle surge forward. He snapped the wheel to the side, avoiding a head-on collision with the line of traffic piled up on the other side of the light.

Behind him Bolan heard another automobile lock up its brakes and their immediate protesting screech as the attempt failed. There was a loud, flat *bang* and the sound of metal crumpling as a driver slammed into the back of the pickup truck. Bolan glanced in his mirror and caught a brief image of an air bag deploying through a cracked windshield.

The steering wheel was rock steady under his grip, and Bolan figured the rear suspension and axle had been undamaged by the glancing blow. He shifted up out of third gear and laid the car open. Setting the mini-Uzi in his lap, Bolan used his left hand to power down the windows on both the driver and passenger sides of his vehicle.

Driving smoothly with one hand, Bolan grasped the mini-Uzi tightly and lifted the weapon. He straight-armed the machine pistol out the driver's window and swerved out from behind a vehicle, putting himself directly behind Kubrick. Bolan triggered a 3-round burst, striking the back window of the agent's car. The rounds slapped onto target, scratching the glass. He triggered another tight burst. The 9 mm rounds struck the window inches from the first burst, scarring the reinforced glass again.

Kubrick twisted hard on his steering wheel, leaping his vehicle into the next lane of traffic. Bolan swerved around another slower moving car and locked on to Kubrick like the rear jet in a dogfight. He rested his forearm against the door frame, steadying his aim. Bolan lined up the muzzle of his machine pistol and triggered a third burst from the weapon.

His rounds struck the rear window of Kubrick's vehicle in the same tight pattern as the first two bursts. The safety glass spiderwebbed in protest under the repeated assaults. Kubrick turned his car sideways at a street corner, using his emergency brake to freeze his rear wheels as he attempted the maneuver. Bolan's foot cut to his brakes and he cranked his wheel at the last moment in order to avoid losing Kubrick as the man initiated a ninety-degree turn on smoking, screaming tires.

A line of civilians on mopeds threw themselves from their little bikes as Kubrick slid around the corner. They scrambled up onto the hoods of parked cars, shouting and screaming, leaving their motorbikes overturned on the street, the wheels still spinning. Kubrick rolled over one, flattening the frame and spinning it curbside.

Bolan revved his engine and his vehicle raced forward, ramming Kubrick's car. Rebounding sharply from the impact, Bolan gritted his teeth and brought his vehicle back on line. Kubrick swerved sharply, fighting to keep his own car under control. Bolan thrust his weapon out of his open window and tore loose with another burst at close range.

The rounds hammered into Kubrick's trunk, which absorbed the damage. The agent swerved his car again, forcing Bolan to follow him. Sweat soaked Bolan despite the temperate weather, and he squinted in concentration. He was bruised and raw from the battle.

Bolan brought his vehicle in behind Kubrick's again. He lowered his weapon and took aim at the other vehicle. He stiffened his arm to hold the machine pistol steady, bracing his grip and wrist against the recoil. With cool deliberation Bolan squeezed the trigger. The gun erupted in his hand.

This time the rounds struck the weakened glass and punched through, leaving fist-sized holes in the rear window. Through the opening Bolan saw Kubrick frantically twisting his steering wheel with one hand while shouting into a cell phone. Bolan triggered another burst but this hit Kubrick's vehicle low, ricocheting off the reinforced materials of the vehicle's trunk.

Kubrick jerked his wheel to the side and Bolan shot forward into the gap, the nose of his vehicle just past Kubrick's passenger-side door. Kubrick saw him in his side view mirror and swerved, slamming hard into the front of Bolan's BMW. Bolan had anticipated the maneuver and cut his own wheel sharply toward Kubrick's car.

The two vehicles clashed hard, rocking the drivers. Bolan jerked his wheel around, turning his tires into Kubrick's vehicle. The agent slammed on his brakes and spun his vehicle away from Bolan's press.

The front of Kubrick's fender tagged another car in the back tire and sent the smaller vehicle spinning. It struck a motorcycle just ahead of it, and the rider was tossed over the handle bars and onto the back of a parked car. The motorcycle went spinning end over end into the plate-glass window of a storefront, sending shoppers scattering for cover.

Strung out perpendicular to the flow of traffic, Kubrick panicked, killing his engine. Leaving his own car running, Bolan popped his engine out of gear and engaged his emergency brake. He heard Kubrick try to turn his ignition over, heard the attempt fail.

Bolan came out of his car in a flash. He leaped into the air and slid over Kubrick's trunk where his own left front fender was locked in tight with the car. As he came down, Bolan heard the other man's engine catch and roar back to life.

The soldier landed on his feet directly behind Kubrick's vehicle. He raised his mini-Uzi and triggered a blast through the blown-out back window as Kubrick kicked his vehicle into Reverse.

Bolan put his burst directly into the back of Kubrick's seat and saw the big man shudder with the impact of the rounds. Then the car lurched backward and Bolan was forced to dive onto his own vehicle to avoid being run down.

The Mercedes missed Bolan by inches and struck the back bumper of the soldier's car, knocking it aside and spilling Bolan onto the pavement. He struck the ground hard, tearing the flesh of his left hand, but he stubbornly refused to release his Uzi machine pistol. Bolan pushed himself up as Kubrick straightened his car. The Executioner didn't have a clear angle into Kubrick's automobile, but fired anyway, cracking the rear passenger window with his burst.

Bullets from Bolan's gun streamed through the back

of Kubrick's car as the man swung it around. They flew wide of the driver's seat and burrowed into the dash. Bolan caught a glimpse of the housing from Kubrick's steering wheel flying apart under the impact of the 9 mm rounds.

Pieces of the steering column housing flew up and Kubrick released the wheel, instinctively covering his face with his hands. The Mercedes swerved out of control and rammed a parked car. The Mercedes rebounded from the impact and stalled, the hood crumpled upward under the impact.

Bolan staggered to his feet and lifted his weapon as Kubrick threw open his car door and struggled out of his vehicle. Twisting, the agent lifted his pistol and pulled the trigger.

Bolan dived and Kubrick's rounds burrowed into the back of the BMW. Rolling over his shoulder, Bolan came up with his weapon ready. Kubrick darted around the front of his car while pedestrians cowered on the sidewalks or fled into shops.

The big agent jerked open the door of a vehicle stopped in the middle of the street. A balding, middle-aged man in a bright yellow track suit shouted something at Kubrick who clubbed him with the butt of the H&K pistol. The man sagged under the impact, and he was pulled out of the car and into the street.

From behind the cover of the car door, Kubrick turned and fired on the maneuvering Bolan, forcing him to dive for cover. Kubrick jumped behind the wheel of the seized car. He accelerated forward, the undamaged vehicle responding well under his hand. Bolan fired a burst at the retreating vehicle, saw a spark fly off the back frame and then twin shatter marks burst on the rear windshield.

All around him people screamed in terror. Chechen rebels had kept up resistance in the mountains, but Grozny had remained largely pacified since the second conflict. The civilians had no idea what to make out of the gun battle. Kubrick was more than a block away and moving fast by the time Bolan made it back into his car.

Bolan shoved his car into gear and cranked it around so that it was pointing in the right direction. He pushed the gas pedal to the floor and drove the car away from the scene. In Kubrick he had found a dangerous opponent as committed as himself.

Bolan assessed the situation. He had a magazine and a half of ammunition left for the mini-Uzi, two for the Glock 17 and one for the Victor High Standard. He was bruised and roughed up but not truly injured. His vehicle had taken some shots and was no longer inconspicuous but still ran well. That by far, along with a choking timetable, was Bolan's greatest worry at the moment.

Kubrick put himself on Vlidstaka Avenue and instinctively Bolan knew the man was cutting for the city's main arterials. That meant Kubrick was heading away from the International District where the Caucasus Data Institute was located. Kubrick had made contact with others and he was attempting to use the confrontation to draw Bolan away from Vesler.

Bolan forced himself to cool his blood. He needed to remain tightly focused on his objective, keep his eyes on the prize. Kubrick was, at the moment, a means to an end and not the end himself. Bolan pushed his car forward, coming closer to Kubrick in his stolen car, forcing the illusion that he still chased him.

The soldier whipped in and out of traffic, trying to close the distance between himself and the other man.

If he could catch a shot before Kubrick made it onto the highway, then Bolan would take it. Otherwise, he would terminate pursuit once Kubrick committed himself to the on-ramp and was locked into a course of action.

Bolan didn't need a situational role reversal with Kubrick tight on him while he tried to beat a second team to the CDI and Vesler.

Three streets whipped past with Bolan hard on Kubrick, but in no position to take a shot. Both of the men drove their vehicles intensely, weaving in and out of slower traffic at nearly suicidal speeds. Bolan realized he was never going to get a good shot at Kubrick and tossed his weapon to the side.

Kubrick turned, crossing into the wrong lane as he passed other vehicles. Bolan followed close behind him. The agent made no attempt at subterfuge in his driving. He simply bullied his way into the right-hand-turn lane and sped toward the freeway on ramp. Bolan followed Kubrick around the corner, feeling the center of his vehicle's gravity shift at his hard cut. He laid off the accelerator and watched Kubrick's speeding vehicle widen the gap between them.

Kubrick, thinking Bolan was right behind him, sped up the on-ramp and thrust himself into traffic. Bolan shot past the freeway entrance. Once past the onramp, drove off the main streets and searched for a fast and convenient place to stash his battered vehicle.

15

Bolan got out of the taxi and paid the driver.

He surveyed the building and grounds of the Caucasus Data Institute as the taxi drove away. The building was made of sturdy, respectable old brick and obviously dated from before the Second World War. It was surrounded by a high chain-link fence with a single security manned entrance off the main street.

Two Russian nationals, in private security uniforms and boasting side arms, directed traffic in and out of the electronically controlled front gate.

Bolan lifted his knapsack to his shoulder and checked traffic before crossing the street. He felt time, like the slow burning fuse of a detonator, burning down on him. At any moment, opposition could come screaming in like dive-bombers. He had tripled the cabdriver's fare to coax the man to excessive speeds, and he felt hopeful that he had made good time—especially if Kubrick's plans were off the books.

Government advice and subsidies, due to the delicate nature of the institute's work, had provided for expensive, if unspectacular, security upgrades. The security booth in front of the electronic gate was bulletproof and camera monitored. The two guards worked the post, checking IDs before opening the remote controlled gate to allow access.

One of the guards looked over at Bolan as he approached the booth. The man made no attempt to open the door as Bolan walked to him. He was built thickly but flabby, with a pockmarked face and a light dusting of dandruff on his navy colored uniform shirt. His partner was a younger, thinner and more hygienic version of the first man.

"Hello. My name is Cooper," Bolan said. "I don't have an appointment. Please alert the receptionist that I'm from the Meltzer Import Export Emporium."

The pockmarked guard stared at him with flat, muddy eyes. He blinked them once, reptilian in composure.

"You understand my Russian?" Bolan asked.

"I understand," the man answered.

"Great. Now. Will you alert the receptionist? Tell her I'm from the Meltzer Emporium."

"I'm sorry, sir, but our protocols are very strict."

"I'm not asking you to let me through the gate without an appointment. I'm asking you to check me in with Mr. Vesler's receptionist."

Bolan kept his face impassive, though at any moment he expected car loads of reinforcements to roar around the corner and gun him down where he stood.

"Mr. Vesler is a very busy man, sir," the guard said.

"That's why I'm asking you to contact his receptionist first."

"This is highly irregular. Perhaps if you had some sort of paperwork for me...." The man's voice trailed off, thick with innuendo.

The younger guard behind him snickered, and Bolan realized he was being shaken down for a bribe. He sighed and then reached reluctantly inside his jacket. The older guard allowed a little smile to play on his rubbery lips, and he slid open the metal door to the security booth.

"I think I have a few papers here that might persuade you," Bolan said. "You don't mind American papers do you?"

"Depends." The man grunted the word noncommittally, but betrayed himself by leaning forward, avarice gleaming in his eyes. The younger guard was grinning openly. He idly picked his nose while he watched the transaction unfold.

Bolan pulled out his wallet, held it open while the older guard's eyes went to it. He dropped it and watched the man's eyes follow the money. Bolan struck like a snake uncoiling.

Reaching out with one bear trap of a hand, Bolan snatched the guard around his wrist. He yanked hard as the man leaned in, snatching the man off his stool. As the guard fell forward, Bolan's left hand struck him hard in the shoulder. He smoothly stepped inside and spun the man, locking his arm up behind his back.

The guard squawked out loud as Bolan shoved him roughly up against the metal-edged door of the booth. The other guard, mouth gaping, leaped to his feet in protest. Bolan smoothly unholstered the guard's Tokarev pistol. The younger man froze, eyes bulging.

"Sit!" Bolan snarled.

The guard sat.

Bolan threw the pistol onto the ground inside the guard station. He shoved the older guard in after his weapon. The man sprawled into the arms of his comrade, who struggled to keep from falling to the ground.

"If I have to get on the phone and call the receptionist myself, and tell her that the gate guards prevented a representative of a valuable client like Meltzer's Emporium from solidifying a contract, there will be hell to play. Now. How are my papers?"

The younger guard scrambled to pick up the phone in the booth. He turned his back on Bolan while the older man retrieved his weapon, a sullen look on his face. As the older guard stood, the other man hung up the phone and turned to face Bolan, his face flushed.

"You may report to the receptionist."

BOLAN PRESENTED HIMSELF before the camera overlooking the front entrance to the institute. He waited a second, then there was a buzz as the lock to the dead bolts were disengaged. He reached out and pulled one of the heavy doors open.

Stepping into the Caucasus Data Institute, Bolan felt a strange sense of arrival. The tangled trail that had started in Garabend's lair had begun here. Secrets had flown out of this place, betrayals and political gambits had been spit out like bills from an ATM. Bolan had picked up the disparate pieces of information, broken lives, bloody fingerprints and followed them all back to this quiet, efficient building.

He looked down the hallway past rows of office doors on either side. At the far end of the hall a skylight had been placed above a solarium and in the center, behind a formidable desk, sat a sharp-eyed receptionist. She glanced up as the door swung closed behind Bolan then returned to typing busily on a PC workstation.

Realizing that he looked nothing like either a research scientist or an executive, Bolan began walking calmly toward the woman. If he could keep her from alerting the Grozny police or sending a security detachment down on him, he thought he'd be doing pretty well. He passed a door marked Sylvia Tan as he made for the reception desk. The office was dark and shut up tight.

Bolan stopped in front of the desk, taking in the plethora of potted plants arrayed around the otherwise rather clinical room. The nameplate read K. Sari. The woman stopped typing and looked up at him. Her looks were classically Scandinavian and pretty in the no-nonsense sort of a way Bolan associated with college professors and intelligence officers. She seemed to be slipping into late middle age with dignity and poise.

"Hello," Bolan said.

Looking over glasses, Ms. Sari took in Bolan's casual dress and the black knapsack slung casually over his shoulder. Bolan could see her deducting points behind her cool exterior. He tried to prevent himself from smiling.

"*You* are from Meltzer's?" she asked.

"Please inform Mr. Vesler that a representative of Mr. Kubrick's is here to speak with him."

Ms. Sari arched a questioning eyebrow at him. Bolan smiled back at her. He was acutely aware of the sinister black eyes of multiple cameras focused on him. He was fairly certain that Vesler had been alerted to his presence upon arrival and was likely looking at him through a closed-circuit TV screen inside his office.

"One moment, please," Ms. Sari said.

She picked up a telephone and punched a number. Her voice dropped to a discreet murmur. Bolan waited patiently as Ms. Sari listened to the response. She placed the handset carefully back into its cradle. She looked up at Bolan over her glasses.

"Mr. Vesler will see you. Please follow me."

Bolan stepped back to give the woman some room as she stepped out from behind her desk. He took the opportunity to admire the way her posterior moved under her fitting, but tasteful skirt.

Ms. Sari smiled perfunctorily and stepped aside as she pushed open a door of dark wood and ushered Bolan into Vesler's office. Bolan nodded agreeably and walked past her. He hoped he wouldn't have to frighten Ms. Sari by beating her supervisor half to death in order to get the information he needed.

The office was a large corner unit with blinds drawn across floor-to-ceiling windows. The room was done in mahogany and leather, with a dark chocolate carpet.

Bolan stepped fully into the office and heard Ms. Sari close the door firmly behind him. Dieter Vesler looked up from behind a desk cluttered with papers, files and computer printouts of schematics and graph charts. Three phones and two computers sat on the desk in front of the man.

Vesler blinked blue eyes behind thick glasses. He stood, rising to an impressive height and extended a big hand at the end of a long thin arm toward Bolan. Vesler wore a white lab coat, complete with a full pocket protector, over a stylish business suit of austere brown and a matching tie. His fingers were blunt, the nails cut short and his silver mustache was thick but carefully trimmed.

Bolan met the firm, dry handshake with his own. The man wore a Rolex Executive watch and a heavy gold signet ring. Vesler appeared to be cosmopolitan and stylish without crossing over into effeminate. He seemed a man unlikely to bend under threats of blackmail, but heavy cocaine habits had made stronger men than him weak in the face of ruthless pressure.

"You are from Kubrick?" His voice was curt, the tone clipped. "Excuse me for being blunt, but I hope you appreciate that I am a busy man."

Bolan nodded and settled into one of the big, comfortable chairs across from Vesler's desk. When he sat down Bolan saw that one of the computer screens showed four separate views from a CCTV security feed, just as he had suspected.

"In a manner of speaking," Bolan answered, waiting for a reaction.

"What does that mean?" Vesler snapped. "I do not have time for games, as I have said. Are you from the emporium?"

"Let's say I'm from the overseas holding company behind the emporium."

"Do you delight in being obtuse?" Vesler asked.

"Not as much as you do in snorting coke."

"I've never—" Vesler's voice was strangled with his outrage and his face had blossomed red in anger.

"If you'd 'never,' then you wouldn't have sold out my country and put the lives of better people than yourself in danger. Now start answering my questions," Bolan said, leaning over the desk.

"You have identification?"

"That won't be necessary."

"How can you expect me to speak!"

"Shut up," Bolan snapped. "I'm not here as a courier. I'm not here to give you security tips, or to strong-arm information out of you because the last hooker you were with took pictures of you snorting coke on her camera phone. Understand?"

Vesler, despite his size, cringed from the more aggressive Bolan. His eyes blinked behind his glasses.

Beads of sweat suddenly broke out across his wide, high forehead like fat raindrops.

"Understand?" Bolan repeated.

"Wh-what?" Vesler stammered, growing redder. "What do you want?" His voice almost reached to a shriek.

"Tell me where Sable is. I won't ask again. Tell me and then get the hell out of here before Kubrick comes for you."

Bolan reached behind him and pulled out his silenced Victor High Standard and set it down on the desk. Any growing indignation Vesler might have been feeling at his rough treatment evaporated instantly.

Vesler moaned and slumped forward in his chair before burying his face in his hands.

Bolan gave Vesler an opportunity to collect himself. He carefully put away the .22-caliber pistol, this time in the front pocket of his jacket. He felt no sympathy for the corrupt man. Vesler's refusal to face his personal demons had put the lives of others in danger.

"It can end with me," Bolan said. "It can end now. Tell me where Sable is, and there'll be no one left to blackmail you. You'll be free." Bolan said.

Vesler looked up, disbelief fighting with hope on his ruddy face. He didn't trust the frightening man before him, but Vesler desperately wanted to believe. He seemed to come to some internal decision, and he straightened in his chair. He ran his hands through his thick, graying blond hair.

Bolan waited impassively for the man to control himself. The clock was ticking. His face was all over CDI security film. Kubrick would know exactly who had been here when he left.

Kubrick would have Vesler talking almost as fast as Bolan had, but the soldier couldn't very well bring himself to kill Vesler just to tie up a loose end. Sanders had turned Vesler into Sable's stringer. The pitiful excuse for a corporate executive had thought himself working under different elements of Western intelligence.

Bolan looked at the video screen displayed on the second of Vesler's two terminals. A gray sedan pulled through the open security gate. For a second the camera panned inside the vehicle, and Bolan quickly counted five men crammed into the midsized economy model.

"Time's up, Dieter. Tell me now or lose the opportunity I'm giving you."

"Fine, fine." Vesler leaned back in his chair.

The German opened his mouth, prepared to speak, and intuition struck Bolan like a lightening bolt.

"Shut up!" Bolan snapped, interrupting a now completely stunned Vesler.

Bolan had almost been fatally foolish in the very moment of his triumph. Agency technicians and countersurveillance specialists probably swept Vesler's office on a regular basis looking for bugs, but such actions were not perfect countermeasures. A parabolic microphone operation pointed at those ceiling-to-floor windows would be a completely passive activity. Bolan could not afford to have Vesler speak the location of Sable out loud.

Bolan looked at the video feed. Five men with short hair, broad shoulders and trim waists were entering the building. On a second of the four video feeds Bolan saw a second car, nearly identical with the first, pulling through the gate. Things were closing in around him rapidly now.

As Bolan's race neared the finish line, his room to maneuver was being strangled. He couldn't leave Vesler in the hands of the crew rolling in through the front doors, even if he wanted to.

"You have your keys?" Bolan demanded.

"What?"

"Your car keys, you have them?"

"Yes, of course, but I—"

"Shut up and stand up, you're coming with me."

"I can't—"

"Tell it to the gun, Dieter."

Bolan leveled the .22 at the stunned man. Vesler's eyes widened to ridiculous proportions behind his thick glasses. The effect would have been almost comical if the situation hadn't been so completely and utterly serious. Desperate, Vesler wrote down the address on a piece of paper and shoved it toward Bolan.

"Here, here, take that, she's there. I swear!"

"No good." Bolan crumpled the paper into his pocket. "Kubrick's sent men to kill you. You either take me to Sable's location or you commit suicide. Your choice, but you have two seconds to make up your mind."

"I'll come with you," Vesler said.

"Good choice."

Bolan looked at the video monitor, saw the hit squad approaching Ms. Sari's desk. He directed Vesler toward the corner of his office farthest from the door.

Bolan whirled and put his foot against his chair, kicking out. The chair lodged with its back under the doorknob. Bolan eyed the camera feed again and then turned his back on both desk and door. Vesler was making confused noises from his position in the corner.

"Pull the blinds," Bolan ordered.

Vesler turned to obey. The Executioner didn't wait for the German to complete his task. As soon as Vesler turned his back, Bolan lifted his pistol and pulled the trigger four times. The sound-suppressed subsonic .22 hollowpoint rounds struck the glass and mushroomed out, splintering the floor-to-ceiling windows.

Vesler gasped at the sound and spun. Bolan reached over and picked up the second leather chair sitting in front of Vesler's desk. He tossed it into the already broken window, shattering the glass completely.

"Go! Get to your car, now," Bolan snarled.

He took a threatening step toward Vesler and the man scrambled to obey. The scientist stepped carefully through the hole. Bolan was behind him instantly, pushing the man forward into the parking lot. As he moved, Bolan slid the .22 pistol into his waistband.

Bolan stayed close to Vesler as he hustled him across the parking lot. He kept one hand on the researcher's elbow and another close by the pistol butt sticking out of his waistband.

"Get your keys out, damn it. Which one is your car?"

"The red Porsche 922, over there in the executive parking lot."

"Of course. Now move."

16

The Caucasus Mountains above Grozny led to the border with Georgia. The area had been the refuge of Islamic rebels after both Chechen conflicts. Russian forces still hunted and skirmished among the valleys with determined insurgents.

It was a place that, unlike the oil infrastructure, hadn't received much in the way of postconflict rebuilding funds. Outside of the city proper, Vesler was forced to slow the Porsche in order to better deal with the unimproved roads.

Bolan quizzed Vesler ruthlessly on the trip but was left discontent with the answers the research scientist gave him. He knew only that Sable operated out of a dacha in the mountains where she paid mercenaries for both protection and privacy. Because his position gave him access to information that had become Sable's main financial pipeline, Vesler had been made privy to the location of her redoubt.

Twilight gathered as Vesler took a labyrinthine route of back roads in order to avoid military and interior police patrols. After turning off the regional highway, the sports car made the climb into the mountains above the city with little trouble.

The road to Sable's dacha was narrow and winding. The area was rough and isolated, giving Sable little in the way of neighbors. After darkness had completely fallen, Vesler stopped at the edge of a gated compound on what appeared to have once been a logging road.

Bolan surveyed the sprawling house behind the wood-and-metal fence. The dacha made Kubrick's house look like a second-rate shack. No guards were in evidence. There was a intercom station with a camera set next to the black metal gate at the end of the drive. Bolan took that in and frowned, deep in thought.

He picked up his GPS unit from the middle console of the sports car. He activated the device and then double-checked his results. Satisfied, he pulled out his BlackBerry and typed in his GPS coordinates. He sent them through a wireless burst transmission before he returned both items to his knapsack.

"Who are you, James Bond?" Vesler sneered, trying to rally his pride with bravado.

Bolan looked up at him casually, face impassive. "What?"

"Nothing," Vesler muttered.

"No, really. I missed it. Say it again."

Vesler paled. "Nothing. I didn't say, anything."

"Drive," Bolan ordered.

"What? But here is—"

"Shut up and drive on," Bolan said.

BOLAN CLEARED THE DACHA'S estate wall and crossed the stretch of back lawn.

The lush, closely cut grass of the landscaped yard ended at a two-foot-high retaining wall, separating lawn from the security wall in the back. Crouch walking,

Bolan kept as low a profile as possible until he had reached the cover of a pruned and sculpted pine tree and large bush near the left-hand side of the fence.

Pulling out his .22, Bolan settled into a comfortable crouch, supporting his arm on a low hanging branch.

He could see the backyard very clearly in all the ambient light the house was throwing out through the picture windows set into the back of the dacha. To the right of his position, across the lawn, was an Olympic-size swimming pool, complete with slide and diving board, drained into an empty, hollow pit. Beyond the pool house were the garage and kennels.

Behind him, Bolan heard the wind moving through the branches of the trees. The pine smell reached his nose. The same breeze driving the smell of pine to him would be picking up his scent and wafting it across the yard toward the dog runs behind the five-car garage. Bolan detected no movement from the well-lit house, but the sound of the stereo playing reached his ears, over the sound of the low wind.

Vesler had said that upon seeing them for the first time, he had promptly dubbed Sable's guard dogs the "terror twins." Less than four minutes after Bolan climbed out from the shelter of the wall two Doberman pinschers trotted out from beside the house. Both dogs kept their noses in the air, searching out the scent carried to them on the soft mountain breeze.

One dog swung his head in Bolan's direction and snarled. The other growled in answer and began trotting toward the deep shadows of the shrubbery.

Bolan hated to kill animals just doing their job, but he had no choice. His pistol coughed and the closest dog went down. The sound-suppressed, subsonic .22 caliber round entered just under its ear, severing the spine and dropping the dog instantly. The other dog barked once in surprise and turned toward his fallen brother. Bolan's shot took him through lung and heart, entering just behind the right foreleg. The black dog folded instantly.

Bolan was on his feet and moving. He crossed the lawn in a fast jog, hoping to be inside long before anyone noticed the motionless dogs.

Halfway across the lawn the soldier passed through an arc of light thrown out by a floodlight set high up on the side of the house. Crossing the beam he went to one knee on the other side, bringing the pistol up in both hands. He took a long, careful moment to sight in on his target before squeezing the trigger with slow, even pressure.

The gun coughed again. The halogen floodlight connected to the proximity sensor exploded. Caution had argued for Bolan to take the shot from the relative safety of the lawn retaining wall, but he didn't have enough faith in the accuracy of the modified weapon across that longer distance. Light neutralized, Bolan rose and sprinted toward his target.

He raced through a flower bed, hurtled a low hedge and landed on a back patio. Weaving his way past metal framed lawn furniture, Bolan gained the back of the house just under the second-story deck. He moved quickly to the left corner of the house.

Slowing his pace, Bolan set his back against the wall. About ten yards down, toward the front of the house, was a secondary door.

Pistol ready, Bolan slid up next to the door. At eye level a relay box for the dacha alarm system burned a passive green. No intruders had been detected, no alert sounded. Bolan's reconnaissance had been as exhaustive as time had permitted. As far as he was able to determine, the protective system did not include remote cameras or pressure sensors.

Bolan quickly inserted his lock pick gun and compressed the lever trigger. He heard the subtle scraping of metal on metal as the prongs manipulated the pins of the lock. The bolt clicked home and the doorknob turned under his hand.

Steeling himself, Bolan entered Sable's lair.

Bolan moved through the door in a sudden, fluid movement, pulling it quickly shut behind him and stepping to one side as he entered the building. His pistol was out in front of him, tracking. The big room was dark, a jumble of hulking, shadowy shapes. Going to one knee, Bolan waited for his eyes to adjust after having his night vision blown by the house lights outside.

His pupils quickly expanded, and he began picking out details. He was in a game room that contained two billiards tables and a massive home entertainment system. Various electronic games and expensive, comfortable-looking furniture were scattered around. Across the massive room from the outside door a short flight of stairs led up to the main floor of the house.

Bolan stood, shifting his knapsack off his back as he did so. With it in hand he crossed the room to the stairs. He could clearly hear music coming from upstairs. He was depending on it to cover any slight noise he made while moving. To his possible detriment, however, it increased his chances of being surprised going through transition points.

Reaching the stairs, Bolan looked up. The door to the next level was tightly closed, a bar of light showing through at the bottom. He mounted the steps, knelt in front of the door and set his pistol down. It took only a moment to remove a fiber-optic camera tactical video system from the knapsack. The borescope had been preassembled, but Bolan still needed both hands to position the surveillance device. He slid the tiny cable under the doorway and then turned on the handheld video display screen. An image of the room on the other side of the door popped up clearly. Bolan smoothly panned the fiber cam across the room.

The great room stretched from the front to the back of the house, with a wet bar along one wall and a sunken leisure area containing costly pieces of furniture and art. The floor was dark hardwood and a spiral staircase ran from the second level to beside the bar. The room appeared empty.

Bolan frowned. Everything about this probe was hasty. Domestic help came cheap in the economic shambles of postconflict Chechnya. Sable could have half a dozen live-in servants rushing around the dacha, fetching her meals and cleaning up after her.

A maid's salary usually wasn't high enough to encourage heroics in the face of armed intruders, but when Bolan acted, he didn't like the idea of various civilians wandering haphazardly through the kill zone. It had happened too often no matter what precautions he took.

Suddenly Peter Sanders stepped around a corner along the same wall as Bolan's door, coming around the end of the wet bar with a drink in his hand. Bile rose in the back of Bolan's throat. Sanders sure didn't look like a man run to ground, in danger for his life. He looked pretty at ease in his surroundings.

Bolan set his mouth in a hard, straight line. This confirmed suspicions that had caused him to enter the dacha on a hard probe in the first place. Sanders was obviously hand in glove with Sable. Sanders was about to get a visit from someone who was there to "rescue" him.

Through the borescope, Bolan watched Sanders walk across the area and step down into the entranceway. The front door opened, and Sable walked into the informal entertaining area. Sanders trailed her, standing close at her side.

They crossed to the bar and Sanders watched as Sable poured herself a drink. While they did this Bolan quickly broke down his surveillance device, secured it in his pack, then removed a stun grenade. Slowly he released his breath, like a pressure valve bleeding steam. He focused himself, mentally imagined each step he was about to execute as clearly and precisely as he could picture. He was like a dancer choreographing a particularly difficult routine. Each step had to be perfect.

Bolan snatched the pin from the flash-bang grenade and let the lever spring free. There was a metallic sound as the coil spring holding the weapon parts together disengaged. The soldier swung open the door and stepped through.

Sanders stood on one side of the bar, his face registering only shock as he froze in midsentence. Sable was spinning, her hand diving toward the small of her back under a designer cut leather jacket.

Bolan lobbed the primed grenade in a gentle underhand, aiming for it to roll across the well-polished top of the wet bar. Sanders's mouth worked like a fish yanked clear of the water. Hands free, Bolan stepped back around the protective corner of the door. He drew a Taser and snapped it on. With his right hand he pulled his Glock.

The grenade's bang was brutally loud and the flash blinding. Sable's stereo system abruptly shut down. Bolan stepped back into the main room from around the corner, pistol held ready, snuggled safely close at his hip. He leaped forward and the Taser came out like the fangs of a cobra as he struck. Sable backpedaled in the face of the sudden, incapacitating flash-bang, arms held up like a person expecting the impact of a car wreck. Sanders collapsed, sagging against the counter behind him.

Bolan took two steps and went airborne. He landed on his hip on the bar and his momentum carried him sliding down its length. He whipped his Taser around and caught Sable in her ribs. The electrical charge locked the woman and then swept her to the ground, her eyes rolling up to show white. She made crude, inarticulate sounds deep in her throat.

As Sable went down, Bolan spun. He cleared the counter, rolling off the edge and came down next to Sanders. The American agent cringed before him, raising his hands and cowering like a child. Bolan snarled and moved forward, weapon held up in each hand.

"Move!" he shouted.

Bolan took half a step forward and kicked Sanders in the hip, shoving him around the corner of the bar. He thumbed off the Taser's power and clipped it onto his belt. Following the stumbling Sanders, Bolan kicked him again, this time driving the man's arm into his side and spilling him onto the floor next to the incapacitated Sable.

Sanders looked up, terrified. He saw Bolan with pistol ready, looming above them, a grim manifestation of justice. Bolan's eyes gleamed in brilliant, angry counterpoints to the emotionless affect of his face. The Agency intelligence officer whimpered in horror. Sable moaned ineffectually at his side.

More quickly than Bolan would have thought possible, Sable began to recover. Bolan stepped past the cowering, ineffectual Sanders and over to the Russian operative. Leaning down, he thrust the muzzle of his pistol into Sable's forehead.

"Am I going to have to shoot you, little girl?"

"What?" Sable was still shaking off the effects of her stunning. "Who—"

"I said, do I have to shoot you?" Bolan let the volume and cadence of his voice climb. He tapped the muzzle of his pistol against the bridge of Sable's nose.

"No." Her voice was surprisingly calm.

Already she was suppressing her fear and disorientation. Her eyes sized up Bolan. Bolan brought up his Taser, clicked it on. The device began to hum and crackle with energy. The predatory look was pushed out of Sable's eyes.

"Okay, both of you get up. Sanders, I'm keeping my gun on you. Understand? You try anything, I shoot you. Sable tries anything, I shoot you. No matter how this plays out, you get shot, understand?"

The man nodded, pale, as he climbed to his feet.

"I can't hear you!" Bolan barked, never taking his eyes off the rising Sable.

"Yes! Yes. I get shot, I understand," Sanders babbled.

"Good, now both of you get into the living room. Sit down on that couch."

With a sniper's eye, Bolan watched them, one frightened, one angry, sink into the couch. He replaced his Taser properly, but kept a wide, glass-topped coffee table between himself and the pair.

"Nice place, Sable," Bolan said, putting a big boot on the table. "Apparently turning people into traitors pays well."

"You're messing up, cowboy," Sanders said. "You're American. Who are you and why are you interfering in my operation?"

"Your operation?" Bolan countered. "From what I've been able to tell, this is Sable's operation."

Sanders's eyes were livid points of hate as he looked Bolan up and down.

"Buddy, I'm going to have the Senate Intelligence Committee so far up your ass that you—"

Bolan lifted his Glock. "It's not that kind of operation," he said. "I'm so far off the books I'm illiterate. You understand what I'm telling you?"

Sanders sat stiff, face flushed. He breathed in hard snorts, nostrils flaring with the effort and his mouth set in a hard, thin line. He kept his eyes on the floor, refusing to look up at Bolan. Beside him Sable sat very still. She was unafraid and the look she gave him was calculating.

Sanders shot a protective glance toward Sable, but the woman was watching Bolan with cool inscrutability. The soldier met her gaze. He didn't break it as he reached around and unlimbered his sat phone. He manipulated the instrument and put it to his ear.

"Bring it home, Jack," Bolan said.

He cut the connection.

"Congratulations," Bolan said to Sable. "The United States government is prepared to accept your offer."

"What!" Sanders made to jump to his feet in sudden outrage.

Bolan reached over and smacked the heel of his palm into the agent's forehead, shoving him back down onto the couch.

"You sit down. You aren't Russian, Sanders. You aren't negotiating anything, understand? You are nothing but a failure. You didn't spin her, Sanders, she spun you. You've got a lot to answer to your country for. Don't cross me."

"You're accepting my offer?" Sable sounded incredulous.

"Yep." Bolan nodded.

"Then why all of this?" The beautiful Russian spy master waved her arms around.

Bolan met her eye and locked into her gaze tightly.

"Because," he said, "we have accepted your offer. You will accept the terms of our agreement. There will be no counternegotiations, there will be no backing out, no thinking about it, no shopping around for a better deal. A helicopter is coming now. You will be getting on that helicopter."

"I see," she said.

"This is outrageous!" Sanders was screaming. "This is extortion, kidnapping!" Sanders grew increasingly frantic. "She has the right to negotiations—"

Bolan plucked his Taser off his belt and turned it on again. "Are you going to keep talking?" he asked.

Sanders choked off his words. His face was flaming red with his indignation. Bolan looked at him, disgusted with what he saw. A man given responsibility by his nation and who had thrown that duty away over an infatuation with a woman.

"Why does Kubrick want you dead?" Bolan asked Sable.

"Because he does what Lich tells him to do."

"You spun Lich." It wasn't a question, not anymore.

Sable fixed him with a level stare. "Years ago. Lich was mercenary before the Wall came down. I protected him from the Kremlin intelligence purges. He was mine. Together we worked the CDI."

"Yeah, I have photos of you working Tan," Bolan countered dryly.

Sable shrugged. "Kubrick, under Lich's orders, counterspun Tan so that she thought she was working for Moscow."

"You had Vesler?"

"From the beginning. However I gave my blackmail information to Lich, who exploited him through other channels."

"Why kill you now if not then?"

"I moved from KGB to SVR to certain influential syndicates—"

"Russian Mafia," Bolan said. "So Lich kept getting paid, I get that. But what happened?"

"She's coming over to our side!" Sanders injected, desperate not to be relegated to irrelevance in front of the beautiful Sable.

Bolan ignored the man.

"What happened?"

"I have been compromised," she admitted simply. "When Vesler moved the Gustav prototype to Garabend through his criminal contacts instead of me, he leaked information that left my position vulnerable. A Federal Witness Protection Program is the only security I have of growing old anymore."

Bolan had no idea what a "Gustav prototype" was. It hadn't been in the intelligence he had received from Brognola before the Garabend takedown. He didn't have time to follow up on this secondary thread.

"So you flipped Ranger Joe here to save your bacon," Bolan surmised, bluffing. "The sale of the Gustav would have made you rich enough to disappear. Vesler screwed that up."

Sanders was scarlet. The veins at his temples were vivid, and the cords of his neck stood out. His mouth worked futilely as his fists clenched and unclenched in his lap. Bolan had no doubt the man wanted to rip him limb from limb. He was unconcerned.

"I made contact with Sanders to circumvent Lich when I needed to come over. Somehow Lich compromised those communications. When we went to The Berliner casino there were operatives waiting. I attempted to use Tan to run interference, only to discover that Kubrick had her equipped with a task force of her own in case I made contact. Sanders was in danger as well—Lich would have us both killed. We had to go underground."

"Sanders is a big boy," Bolan said. "He should have kept trying to contact supervision, not play nursemaid to you."

"Your government will be happy with the terms of our trade," Sable answered.

"But not Lich."

"But not Lich," she agreed. "When I'm interviewed, Lich will be a dead man walking."

Bolan grunted. It felt somehow anticlimactic. He had chased this pair from one end of the corrupt, violence filled miasma of Grozny to the other. He had killed, perpetrated violence, followed clues and scraps of clues, risking his life and that of others to get to them. Now he had them and the run was almost over. Had there been a time when he hadn't been worried about Sanders? What he had thought of as a fellow operative in need had turned into a love struck cretin.

The whole thing left Bolan disgusted. Sable was still of tremendous value, but his righteous indignation at Sanders's fate had been a waste of emotion. He shook his head.

"Tell me about the Gustav," Bolan said.

"I sent an emissary to Garabend," Sable replied. "It turned out the son of a bitch had sold me out to Lich.

My man tried to get the prototype but failed. Lich has the Gustav and always did—not me."

Before Bolan could say anything his sat phone chirped. He plucked it off his harness and answered it. He cocked his head to the side and regarded the two operatives on the couch while he listened to the voice on the phone.

"Come in from a south, southeast approach," Bolan instructed. "The lawn to the back of the house is open enough for you to land inside the walls, easily. There are three of us, the bird will have no problem. It's an in-and-out extraction."

Sanders and Sable couldn't hear the reply, but Bolan lowered his pistol and grunted his acquiescence into the phone unit before flipping it shut and securing it.

"You ready?" he asked Sable.

"Always."

"Good. I've got a Black Hawk coming into your backyard right now. If you want a clean pair of underwear or a photo of Mom, get it now. This would be a lot better if I could trust your boyfriend to cover you for his country, but since I can't, we'll all go."

"I've had just—" Sanders began.

From outside the group heard three muted pops like the sound of fireworks going off. The security monitor began to blare. Bolan turned toward the alarm, his eyes searching for the display screen from the CCTV feed. On the screen, like an episode of some television police drama, Bolan saw Sable's gates hanging, blown off their moorings and black SUVs speeding through the breech.

"Kubrick," Sable and Bolan said together.

"Weapons?" Bolan demanded.

"I've been ready for rivals for a while," Sable replied as she rose off the couch.

Sanders popped up like a dutiful jack-in-the-box, prepared to fight fiercely for the woman he felt himself charged with protecting. Bolan restrained himself from shooting the man out of pure irritation.

"Follow me, quickly," Sable said. "I'll show you where my weapons are."

19

"I have an AKS in the trunk of the Land Rover in the garage," Sable instructed. "I have a Bizon-19 under the bar and a couple of handguns around the house."

Bolan looked back at the security camera and then at his watch, rapidly calculating. He looked at Sable and then over to Sanders. He nodded once, curtly, to Sable before turning to Sanders.

"You know the house, I don't. Cut through to the garage and get the AKS. Meet Sable down in the game room. The Black Hawk is coming down in the backyard. My pilot can put it down between you and the hitters, using the minigun. Arm yourself with the pistols, go to the back lawn and hold off Kubrick's team until the helicopter comes."

"What will you do?" Sable asked.

"I'll use the Bizon to keep them back from the house, slow their advance."

"You're willing to protect me?" Sable asked.

The Executioner looked at her. "You are a means to an end, an advantage for my country, a means to defeat people who would kill innocents in my country. That's something I'll fight for. Don't confuse my sense of duty with anything else."

Sable regarded the big man. She met his flat gaze boldly, then nodded. She turned from him and looked at the security monitor set into the wall beside her front entrance.

"They're on the front drive," she said.

"Give me the Bizon," Bolan replied.

Sable raced to the bar and went behind it. She reached under the countertop and slid open a compartment. Her eyes were locked with Bolan's as he stood watching her, his pistol up. They held each other's eyes momentarily, then Sable looked down. The female mercenary pulled her Russian submachine gun from its cubbyhole and jerked back the bolt receiver, chambering a round.

She looked over at Bolan who still watched her, apparently at ease. Kubrick's team had approached close enough that the sound of squealing tires and slamming doors could be heard from the drive before the main doors to the dacha.

Sable thrust her arms out and threw the submachine gun in an easy lob to Bolan. He caught the weapon with one hand, never taking his eyes off the dangerous woman. He holstered his pistol, checked the feed on the submachine gun. He looked back up. Sable placed a spare magazine on the bar.

"Go," he said. "I'll hold them back."

He turned his back to her and walked toward the elaborate sitting area where he had used his pistol to pin Sanders and Sable to the couch only minutes earlier. He flicked the light switch as he moved into the room to avoid silhouetting himself. He lifted the Bizon-19 and sprayed the big picture windows facing the front of Sable's property.

There was a chorus of answering shouts and a volley of gun fire erupted outside, initiating a storm of lead that tore into the room. More glass from the windows shattered. The heavy drapes jerked and danced like puppets as they were shredded. After his initial burst Bolan dropped to the floor, directing his momentum over a shoulder and rolling clear of the room, keeping below the hail of gunfire.

The Executioner slid around the column between sitting room and the entranceway. He looked up at the monitor and saw the three SUVs had been parked to keep the heavy engine blocks between the hit squad and gunfire from the house. Operatives fired at the house from around every protective angle offered by the vehicles.

Bolan spotted Kubrick. The rogue agent was armed with a black machine pistol. The arm that Bolan had savaged during their fight was in a sling and wrapped to his torso. Kubrick held his weapon and gestured wildly, shouting orders at his death squad. From the rear of one of the SUVs a man ran forward, Kalashnikov assault rifle slung over his shoulder and across his back.

The man went to one knee and leveled an RPG-7 at the front of the dacha. Rising, Bolan turned and sprinted. The 2.3 kg 84 mm warhead could penetrate twelve inches of steel armor and would blow through even a reinforced door with ease. Bolan scrambled across the floor and leaped into the air.

Bolan struck the top of the bar and slid across as a fireball blew the front doors off their hinges and rolled into the room like a freight train. He knocked the spare magazine to the ground under him.

Shrapnel and jagged chunks of wood lanced through the air. The mirror and crystal ware on the counters behind Bolan shattered and glass rained down on him like hail. Liquor bottles exploded like bombs, and alcohol poured in torrents from the shelf.

Bolan scooted up to the edge of the bar that provided him with an angle on the front door. He slid the extra Bizon magazine into a cargo pocket. He took the Russian submachine gun in both hands and lined up the open sights toward the burning entranceway. His ears still rang from the explosive concussion and his face bled from a dozen minor lacerations, but his hand was steady on the trigger as gunmen rushed through the front door.

Bolan aimed for the head as they charged, knowing it likely that neither Kubrick nor Lich would have lacked the resources to provide their teams with proper armor as well as weapons. Mercy was a concept of leisure. As the assassins came on, Bolan met lethal violence with lethal violence.

The first shooter breached the door, assault rifle up and at the ready. Bolan put him down with a triple-hammer burst of 9 mm rounds from his submachine gun. The combatant hit the burning floor. The man running in behind him looked down at the point man. He looked back up, searching for a target, and Bolan blew off the left side of the man's face.

The third man in the line tripped up with the second man's falling corpse. Bolan used a burst to scythe the man to the ground and then put a single shot into the top of his skull. Through the swirling smoke and angry screams Bolan saw a round, black metal canister arch into the room.

The soldier rose to his hands and knees as the grenade hit the floor inside the house and bounced toward him. Leaving the Bizon were it lay, he dived forward, scooping up the bouncing hand grenade. His hands wrapped around the black cylinder.

Bolan hit the floor hard from his short hop, absorbing the impact with his elbows. He rolled over and thrust his arm out, sending the grenade shooting away from him. It cleared the corpses in the entranceway and bounced out the front doors. Bolan heard a sudden outburst of curses in Russian as he buried his head in his arms. The grenade went off.

A cloud of smoke billowed in through the doorway on the heels of the concussive force. The Executioner got to his feet, scooping up the Bizon submachine gun. He shuffled backward and crouched behind the bar, heading for the door to the staircase down to the game room. Bolan caught a flash of movement and spun toward the blown-out windows of the sitting room off Sable's main entrance.

He saw two men in khaki jackets rush up to the shattered windows, holding assault rifles. Bolan beat the men to the trigger and his submachine gun spit flame. It recoiled in his hands and shell casings spilled across the floor.

Bolan put two rounds into the face of the first man, bloody holes the size of dimes appeared, slapping the man's head back. Blood sprayed in a mist behind his head and he slumped to the ground, his weapon clattering at his feet.

The soldier shifted to the second gunman. They fired simultaneously. The muzzle-flash of the attacker's weapon burst into a flaming star pattern. The sound of the heavier caliber assault rifle firing was thunderous compared to the more subdued sound of Bolan's 9 mm subgun.

The 7.62 mm rounds tore into the molding of the wall to Bolan's right. Fist-sized chunks from the wall and door frame flew, spilling white plumes of chalky plaster dust into the air.

Bolan's burst hit the man in a tight pattern. The 9 mm bullets drilled into the receiver of the rifle, tearing it from the stunned gunner's hands. Two more rounds punched into his chest three inches above the first. Bolan triggered two rounds into the gunman and took him down, blowing the back of his neck out.

The Executioner danced to the side and grabbed the knob and swung the stair door open.

A gunman came around the corner of the entranceway, weapon up and firing. Bolan put a burst into his knee and thigh, knocking the screaming man to the floor. He put a double tap through the top of his head. Another pair of gunmen rounded the corner from the front entrance. The soldier threw himself belly down, his legs trailing out behind him on the stairs, angling his body so he was out of sight from the shooters in the entranceway.

He swept his submachine gun in a wide loose arc, spraying bullets at the gunman firing through the shattered picture windows. One of the men's weapons suddenly swung toward the ceiling, and Bolan caught a glimpse of him staggering into the darkness.

Bolan lay on the stairs, only his arms and shoulders emerging from the door to the stairwell. He rotated up onto his right shoulder to get an angle of fire on the entranceway. One of the Russian gunmen raced forward and he shot at the man's ankles, bringing him to the floor. Bolan fired another burst into the prone man, finishing him off, only to have his bolt lock open as his magazine ran dry.

Bolan let the Bizon dangle across his chest as another hitter leaped over the body off the first and charged forward. The skeletal, folding stock of his AKS-74U was pressed tight into his shoulder, and he fired the weapon as he bounded toward Bolan.

The Excutioner put his hands against the floor and snapped up, clearing the edge of the doorway. Bullets tore into the floor where his head had just been. He twisted on the stair and jumped down.

A burst of gunfire echoed in the stairwell and 5.45 mm rounds tore into the floor where Bolan had landed. The big American went up against the wall at his back and pulled the 9 mm Glock 17 from its holster. He heard boots thundering on the stairwell and he bent, swiveled and thrust his gun arm around the corner. He triggered four shots without exposing himself.

A gunman pitched forward and bounced down the stairs. He spilled out at the bottom, sprawling in front of Bolan and his weapon skidded out from his hands. Bolan snatched the fallen weapon.

He holstered his pistol and quickly ducked his head into the stairwell before thrusting the carbine around the corner to trigger a burst. Using the covering fire to keep the enemy back, Bolan dragged the dead man at the bottom of the stairs to him by his belt.

He pulled a Soviet-era RGD-5 antipersonnel hand grenade from the man's web harness. He held his Kalashnikov by the pistol grip and stuck out his thumb. Using his free hand to help hook the pin around his extended thumb, he made a tight fist around the pistol grip of the assault rifle and pulled with his other hand, releasing the spring on grenade.

Bolan let the spoon fly. He turned and put a warning

burst down the hall fronting the game room, through the side door. He counted down three seconds and then chucked the grenade around the corner and up the stairs. He turned away from the opening as the blast was funneled by the walls up and down the staircase, spraying shrapnel in twin columns.

Ears ringing, Bolan made for the door to the house. The door hung open, broken. From outside he heard gunfire as the enemy force engaged Sable and Sanders. A figure darted past the open door and Bolan gunned him down.

The Executioner could see the gradual incline running beside the dacha toward the front of Sable's property. He saw men taking positions at the corner of the house, and he fired a burst to keep them back.

A killer flopped onto his belly and threw a bipod-mounted 7.62 mm RPK machine gun in front of him. Bolan jerked back inside the doorway as the machine gunner opened up with the weapon's 660 rpm rate of fire, sending a firestorm in Bolan's direction.

Seeing no movement from the staircase, he turned and looked at the glass doors to the patio on the back lawn. Shrapnel and stray rounds had broken much of the glass, leaving jagged openings. He saw the muzzle flash of gunfire from the back wall where Sable and Sanders held their positions.

He checked the side door to the downstairs and saw woodchips fly off in great, ragged splinters from the withering machine-gun fire. He heard the staccato beat of the weapon discharging. Sensing something, he twisted toward the staircase. A khaki-clad man with a beard rushed off the stairs.

Bolan had the drop on him and gunned him down,

stitching a line of slugs across the Chechen gunman's chest. The man's heel caught on the sprawled arm of a downed compatriot and he tumbled over, dead before he struck the ground.

Bolan scrambled back from the staircase, dodging tables and furniture in the game room. He saw a flash from the stairs and felt the heat as rounds blew by his face. He fired wildly behind him for cover as he rolled across a pool table to land on the other side. He swung back around and covered the staircase and the side door, prepared to send a volley in either direction. His finger tensed on the smooth metal curve of the trigger.

There was a lull in the firing for a moment, and Bolan heard Kubrick screaming instructions in flawless Russian.

"Forward! Forward!" Kubrick shouted.

Bolan stood and made to turn toward the blown-out windows facing the back lawn off the game room. As he rose from his crouch behind the pool table, dark ovals flew down the stairs.

He threw himself flat as the grenades landed in succession on the ground past the corpses of dead rebels. The twin blasts were deafening and shrapnel whizzed through the air. Bolan knew a team would be rushing down the stairs after the grenade blasts, and he fired a ragged burst up the stairwell through the billowing plumes of dirty smoke.

He heard an all too familiar sound and turned as a third hand grenade bounced in. Again Bolan threw himself down behind the pool table as the grenade exploded. Behind him the plasma screen television caught a stray round and exploded in a shower of sparks.

Bolan tucked himself into a ball under the lip of the heavy pool table. He rose out his crouch slightly and set his muscular shoulder against the rim. As close as the fire teams were to his position, Bolan knew he'd never make it across the lawn to where Sable and Sanders fought. This place was his last stand.

Bolan thrust up, pushing against the floor with his legs and heaving his back into the lift. The slate pool table was extremely heavy, and he gasped at the solid weight of the thing. He grunted savagely and pushed harder. The pool table crashed over onto its side with a profound bang and brightly colored billiards balls spilled out of the pockets and rolled wildly across the floor.

The Executioner shifted around to one side of his barricade. He heard boots pounding on the floor a heartbeat before a weapon blast and then the sound of rounds striking the upended pool table.

Bolan rolled onto his stomach and looked around the side of his makeshift barricade. He saw a clean shaved man in the now too familiar khaki uniform reaching down to check a gunman at his feet. Bolan put the man down with a single squeeze of the trigger.

A gunman came through the outside door, weapon up and firing for cover as he made the hostile entry. His wild burst passed over Bolan's head, and the Executioner returned fire with deadly accuracy.

As Bolan spun a hand grenade came lobbing gently over the top of the table and bounced at his feet.

The Executioner dived around the edge of the overturned pool table, desperate to put the big structure between himself and the exploding grenade. Bolan was still in the air when the bomb went off, and he was knocked flat by the force of the detonation.

He hit the floor hard and heard the lurching bang as the billiard table was picked up and then dropped by the force of the explosion. The huge, heavy table soaked up the grenade shrapnel, protecting Bolan even as it was ruined. The soldier rose, feeling dizzy and slightly disorientated.

He sensed movement in the smoke and whirled to fire in that direction. He felt more than saw a man go down, and then he turned and stumbled toward the broken patio windows. He heard noise from the sat phone on his web harness, and then Grimaldi's voice projected over the microphone.

"I'm coming in, Striker."

"This is Striker, copy, Black Hawk. I'm coming out of the house now. I have a visual. Tell your door gunner that everything in the house is hostile. Copy?"

"Good copy. I got eyes on you now, Striker."

"I'm glad to hear you say that," Bolan answered.

He raced out of the house and looked up to see the

helicopter landing on Sable's back lawn. To the embattled Bolan it was as if avenging angels were coming from on high to rescue him.

Underneath the landing gear Bolan saw Sanders and Sable rise out of their positions to make for the chopper. An unknown special operator in a visor helmet and generic OD green jumpsuit manned the helicopter's minigun.

Bolan made for the aircraft, running low, head down even as he heard automatic weapons fire open up from behind him. The door gunner spun the machine gun and unleashed hellfire on the stylish dacha and the gunmen inside. A sheet of flame extended from the rotating muzzles and tore into the house, shredding walls and blowing out windows.

Bolan saw Sanders shove Sable into the helicopter cargo bay and scramble in after her. Bolan ran at an angle to keep clear of the door gunner's line of fire. From the side of the bullet-riddled house the Chechen hardman with the RPK came around the corner.

Bipod still extended down on the squad weapon, he triggered a blast at the helicopter. Sparks flashed as rounds struck the fuselage and the man walked his rounds up the length of the armored special operations model helicopter.

The door gunner responded to the fire by swiveling the minigun to face the new, aggressive threat. His rounds clawed through the house and tore up gouts of earth before smashing into the hardman with brutal velocity.

His finger still on the trigger, the man was knocked off his feet and tossed to the ground. His last burst sent rounds skipping up into the rotor blades of the Black Hawk before the big weapon fell from his lifeless fingers.

Bolan scrambled into the cargo hold of the helicopter, slid across the floor and grabbed a seat strut. Grimaldi looked back into the bay from his seat and smiled when he met Bolan's eyes. The soldier slipped his 9 mm pistol away and gave his old friend a thumbs-up. The aircraft shifted as Grimaldi prepared to pull the bird out of the hot landing zone.

The minigun went silent as the door gunner slumped behind it and fell out of the open cargo door. Bolan lunged for the man but missed as the Black Hawk suddenly lurched. He heard bullets like angry hornets rip through the open door and strike the inside of the helicopter.

From his belly Bolan looked out the open helicopter door at Sable's nearly demolished house. He saw Kubrick lowering the RPK machine gun he'd taken from the fallen hardman. The rogue intelligent agent's face was twisted with a savage satisfaction. Beside Kubrick another man was already on one knee, a grenade launcher snug against his shoulder.

Rounds ricocheted off the armored seats and swing out panels back into the troop transport area. Sable screamed as a white hot round creased her leg on the outer thigh. Sanders threw himself toward the wounded Russian woman, and more tracer fire poured in directly over his back.

Grimaldi finished his swing so that the helicopter's nose was aimed toward the fence at the rear of Sable's dacha property. Bolan looked back, still on his belly, and saw the man beside Kubrick fire his rocket-propelled grenade. It shot out in a streak like a sluggish bolt of lightning and struck the Black Hawk in its tail rotor, shaking the whole aircraft frame.

Bolan looked at the cockpit and saw blood spurt from Grimaldi's shoulder. The veteran pilot rocked from the impact of the round but kept fighting with his controls to keep the Black Hawk on course.

For a moment Bolan thought Grimaldi was going to pull it off.

Another tracer round burned past Bolan's face and clipped the reinforced pilot's seat.

Suddenly the helicopter swung wildly around, and it was sickeningly obvious that the pilot was no longer in control of the helicopter. Bolan felt the bottom drop away beneath him and he knew the helicopter was going down.

He grabbed hold of the seat strut again and spread himself wide on the floor to absorb the impact. The downward pointing nose of the Black Hawk cleared the top of the fence surrounding Sable's dacha by mere inches, and then the helicopter spun wildly to the side.

Bolan heard Sable screaming in Russian, heard Sanders screaming Sable's name. He caught a glimpse of the battered dacha before the fence obscured his view.

Half a heartbeat later the Black Hawk hit.

The belly of the bird slammed into the ground as the rotor blades tore into trees. With a wrenching sound of twisting metal the already weakened rotorhead mechanism, designed to come apart on impact, cut loose from the mainframe of the helicopter and went spinning into the woods.

Bright flickers of yellow flame appear from the nose of the helicopter and Grimaldi slumped forward loosely, hanging against his seat restraints. Bolan pushed himself up and looked over at Sanders and Sable. The impact had knocked the ex-Soviet agent unconscious, but Bolan could detect the rise and fall of her chest as Sanders struggled to get her into a sitting position.

Bolan reached out and grabbed the pilot seat, noting the huge tears where machine-gun rounds had struck. Using the seat as a brace, he pulled himself forward. Blood was pooling in the unconscious pilot's lap from two bullet wounds in his right shoulder. The smell of burning rubber and mechanical fluids was sickening in the confined space of the cockpit. Bolan knew the bird could take a hard landing from as high as sixty-five feet and that the fuel system was self-sealing, so he wasn't worried about the downed helicopter bursting into flames, at least in the next few minutes.

Bolan felt Grimaldi's pulse but it was rapid, weak and fluttering, indicating a frantically beating heart struggling to make up for a reduced blood volume. The man was bleeding to death.

The soldier knew the clock was counting down on him. Kubrick had to be organizing his forces to cross the back lawn and penetrate the wooded hills where the Black Hawk had gone down. Sanders was saying something behind him, but Bolan ignored the man and snatched up the helicopter's radio control.

"Aviary this is Striker, over."

The radio responded instantly. "Striker this is Aviary, go ahead."

"We are down, repeat bird down. Pilot needs medevac. We have a squad of hostiles en route to our twenty, over."

There was moment of silence. Bolan waited for what seemed entirely too long before another voice came over the radio.

"Striker, this is Aviary actual, over," the voice said,

indicating that the command officer of the mission was speaking.

"Go ahead Aviary actual," Bolan replied.

"We are not prepped for secondary extraction."

"I understand. Inform my sponsorship I will be in contact at earliest convenience, per protocol," Bolan said.

The operational support contingent for Bolan had, by necessity been limited. Grimaldi and a crew of task force veterans working under DNI control had been staged on a refitted commercial oil freighter in the Caspian. As a last-ditch fail-safe, two F-22 Raptors staged out of Incirlik air base in Turkey had been scrambled for overflight during the extraction.

"Copy, Striker, good luck."

"Striker out."

His eyes trailed over the cockpit instrument panel. He made sure the bird's GPS locator was functioning. When the Raptors flew over the area, their missile guidance systems would lock on to the signal and vaporize any evidence of U.S. equipment on Chechen soil. If Bolan didn't get Grimaldi and Sable out of there fast, they would all be vaporized.

Assuming Kubrick's hit squad didn't finish them first.

Bolan quickly grabbed a med kit. He found what he was looking for and pulled it free. Putting the packet to his lips, he bit down and tore it open.

Bolan turned and began dumping anticoagulation powder on Grimaldi's wounds. Even in the dim, uncertain light inside the crashed helicopter's cockpit, the man looked deathly pale. He murmured something Bolan didn't catch and then fell silent.

"You've got to help me!" Sanders shouted from the back. "They've breached the fence! Sable's hurt."

"Return fire with the mini," Bolan ordered. "Once I finish giving the pilot first aid, I'll help you fix the woman."

"No! Damn it! Sable is the one who's important, do you understand? That pilot knew the risks, now leave him and help me!"

Bolan twisted and whipped out his pistol. He snatched the startled, frantic Sanders by his collar and shoved the muzzle of his weapon into the man's face hard enough to split his lip. Sanders squawked in protest. He yanked the man closer, and Sanders looked up into the cold blue flint of the Executioner's eyes. He knew he was looking into the eyes of a superior man.

"You want to save your girlfriend?" Bolan whispered. "You do exactly as I say. If you question me again, I'll kill you where you stand. Do you understand?"

Sanders nodded. The motion caused his teeth to click against the hard metal of the pistol muzzle, and he winced in pain.

"Say it!" Bolan snarled. "Do you understand?"

"Yes, yes, I understand," Sanders babbled.

"Good, now get on that gun and keep them off us until I'm done! Go!"

Bolan shoved Sanders in the direction of the minigun and turned to Grimaldi. The pilot was still unconscious and needed more first aid than Bolan could provide for him in the field, but his bleeding had stopped for the moment.

He pulled out his knife, lifted the straps of the seat restraints and cut Grimaldi free of his flight harness.

Automatic weapons fire began to strike the downed aircraft's frame. Despite being shot down, Bolan still felt fairly confident in the helicopter's armor protection from small arms. If not for the inbound Raptors, he might have tried to fight off the attackers, he had to get away from the wreck before it was sanitized by missile fire.

Sanders opened up in retaliation with the mounted minigun. The substantial sound of the weapon was reassuring.

Ignoring Sanders and the incoming rounds, Bolan kept working steadily. He pulled the injured Grimaldi from his seat and laid him out on his back on the floor of the helicopter. He moved farther into the troop transport area and pulled the injured Sable around as well.

The woman's eyes fluttered as he did so and she struggled to rise, confused. Firmly Bolan put a hand on her shoulder and pushed her back down.

"Easy," he said. "Let me stop the bleeding in your leg, and then we'll get out of here."

"Where's my weapon," she asked weakly.

"It must have been tossed clear when we hit," he replied.

Bolan pulled out his pistol and pressed it into her hand. She took it, gratitude showing on her face. Bolan used his knife to slit open the leg of her pants. He set the knife aside and tore the fabric free, ignoring Sable's moan.

He pulled a second packet of coagulation powder out and tore it open. He sprinkled a liberal amount on Sable's wound and then quickly wrapped a pressure dressing around it. He tied it off and looked at the woman.

"You want morphine?"

She shook her head as she pushed herself into a sitting position. "I can't afford to have my alertness compromised."

"Good, slide out and make for the woods before Kubrick surrounds us. We have to move. There's a sanitation strike coming any minute."

She nodded and rolled onto her hands and one knee, trailing the hurt leg straight behind her.

Rounds sliced the air above their heads as they maneuvered inside the downed helicopter. Sable slipped out the side cargo door and Bolan followed her. Once his feet hit the ground he turned and pulled the unconscious Grimaldi to him.

"Let's go!" he shouted at Sanders.

The CIA agent had gamely manned the machine gun, attempting to use controlled bursts to save ammunition but also bring the suppressive effect of his superior rate of fire and heavier caliber into play. Sanders and saw Bolan hoist Grimaldi over his shoulder as Sable hobbled toward the tree line.

He immediately spun away from the machine gun and slid across the floor of the cargo bay and out the open door. He raced away from the downed helicopter. Bolan was just ahead of him, muscling through the underbrush with Grimaldi.

Bolan saw Sable reach the temporary shelter of a fallen log and slide behind it. The Russian operative turned and brought up the pistol Bolan had given her, ready to cover the running men, though the range was extreme to the point of futility.

Bolan charged forward, working hard until he reached the log. He used his free hand to keep his balance as he slid over the top of the downed tree with the pilot still on his shoulder.

Behind them Kubrick urged his men forward. A hand grenade exploded by the nose of the helicopter, and a three-man fire team charged the cargo bay from the tail of the helicopter. Their weapons raked the helicopter with fire as they assaulted the aircraft.

Bolan pulled out his Victor High Standard. He rested his arm on the trunk of the fallen tree to steady his aim. Sanders leaped across the top of the log and landed heavily on the other side. The first of the Russian mercenaries cleared the door of the Black Hawk. Kubrick, still packing the RPK one-handed, shouted something and more men emerged over the fence of the dacha.

Bolan calculated the distance to the downed helicopter from their position among the rocks behind the fallen tree. He realized that even an optimistic calculation put the ragtag band of wounded operatives too close to the wreckage.

"Come on, we're too close!" he said to Sanders. "Help her, we've got to get away!"

Sanders didn't question his orders. He turned and helped Sable drape her arm around his neck. Bolan hoisted Grimaldi and began to move rapidly over the broken ground, down a short incline and into a brush-choked ravine. Sanders and Sable passed them. Bolan was panting as he struggled to put a fold in the topography between themselves and what he knew was coming.

He never heard the Raptors, but seconds later the bombs struck.

The concussive force was devastating. A gigantic flash of flame materialized, turning night into day and the ground under The Executioner's feet shook hard enough to knock him down. Dirt and rocks rained down around them. As he fell, Bolan tried to throw himself over the helpless Grimaldi and protect him from falling debris.

For a second all the oxygen in the area was sucked up by the explosion, and Bolan gasped to breathe. Spots appeared before his eyes, and then in an instant it was over. Waves of heat rolled past him, leaving him cold in the sudden aftermath of their passing. He kept himself over Grimaldi, holding his head in his arms.

When the detritus stopped falling Bolan risked a look. He lifted his head in time to see the fireball from the explosion roll up into the sky and then dissipate. A column of black smoke, deeper than the night, roiled up from the burning oil slick that was all that remained of the downed helicopter.

Bolan pushed himself to his feet and looked at the flame center. There was a huge crater where the wreckage had been. He knew the Russian government in Grozny would strongly suspect that this had to be American work, but it was unlikely they would ever be able to prove it.

He heard Sanders groan and looked over in time to see the CIA agent pick himself up from where he had blanketed himself over Sable. The woman looked shaken, but still together, under control. Sanders helped the Russian woman to her feet, then turned to survey the damage.

"Jesus," he muttered.

The way the man said it made Bolan think that it might, truly, have been a prayer. Bolan saw no one moving, heard no screams. It seemed the strike had vaporized not only the Russian mercs, but their paymaster, Kubrick, as well. But the Executioner didn't intend to leave it to speculation.

Bolan turned to Sable. "You okay?" he asked.

She nodded. "I'm fine."

"Good. We've got to get moving. That will bring every army and special police unit in the region in a hurry. We have to be long gone by the time they get here."

"Agreed," Sanders said, attempting to insert himself into the conversation.

Bolan ignored him. "I came up through this area to infiltrate your estate. The road is only about a hundred fifty yards from here, but my car is too small to hold all of us."

"It would be easier to take one of mine," she agreed.

"Right." Bolan nodded. "I'm going to do damage assessment, attempt to verify that Kubrick is dead, if possible. If Sanders hurries, he can get your Land Rover down to where I have a car parked."

"I'm not leaving her alone with you!" Sanders shouted.

Bolan was on him before the man could blink, much less perceive that a threat was coming. The soldier simply brought a hard fist straight into Sanders's nose.

The CIA agent went sprawling, arms flapping wildly. He fell, and Bolan heard the man's breath rush from him on impact with the unforgiving ground. Sanders moaned, confused and disorientated from the strike.

The Executioner moved forward and stood over the man. He stepped up and put one big boot across the struggling man's throat. His face was granite hard as he pressed down, cutting off the agent's ability to breathe.

"You're a real slow learner, Sanders. Next time it's a bullet."

Sanders grasped Bolan's foot with his hands and tried to wrestle it free. It was a futile attempt. The intelligence agent gasped and spittle flew from his mouth as his face turned red.

Bolan looked at Sable to see how she was responding to his field discipline. She stood off to the side, unmoving. Her eyes were bright as she regarded Bolan. Her chest moved quickly, rising and falling as she watched the violence, her lips slightly parted. She made no move to help her former contact.

Under Bolan's heel Sanders ceased struggling. The agent was nearly unconscious. Bolan stepped off his throat and the man sucked in a huge breath. The tread mark from Bolan's boot was vivid on the man's neck. Sanders's hands flew to his throat. He sputtered and coughed as he tried to rise.

"Get the Land Rover. Meet us down the road where the red Porsche is parked," Bolan said.

"Vesler's?" Sable asked.

"Yes." Bolan nodded, watching Sanders as the agent struggled to his feet.

"Where's Vesler? Surely you didn't trust him?" Sable said.

"He's in the trunk. He must have alerted Kubrick by some means I don't know about. Why he never led Kubrick to you before I showed up, I have no idea."

"Kubrick suspected Vesler knew where Sable was when she first went underground. He was planning on having Vesler's car tagged," Sanders said. "I was supposed to do it, but Sable contacted me first. Kubrick must have had it done before you got hold of Vesler. You led him right to Sable!"

Bolan looked at the man, saw the fear in his eyes. "If you had done your job and reestablished contact with your out-of-region control, that Black Hawk would not have been forced to come into a hot LZ, the gunner wouldn't have died and my friend wouldn't be laying here comatose. Now shut up and go get that goddamn Land Rover."

"What if Kubrick left security with his vehicles?" Sanders asked.

"Then I'll hear the shots. Now go before I shoot you myself," the Executioner replied.

Sanders looked over at Sable, chagrin showing on his face. The operator met his eyes with a level gaze. He looked away, shot a hate-filled glance at Bolan and began moving through the blast area toward the dacha.

"What's your plan?" Sable asked.

"I need to see if I can ID Kubrick. You check my friend and do what you can. After I radio back damage assessment we'll start down the hill toward the road."

"From there?"

"We head for the Georgian border. I have contacts who will make sure we get out."

"I have a contact with an arms merchant who moves weapons across the border for the Chechen insurgents. He might be able to arrange transport or a secure landing zone."

"I'm not trusting Chechen terrorists. They'd kill Americans in a New York minute."

"Not insurgents, weapons dealers."

"No way," Bolan said.

"Your friend needs medical attention, and quickly."

"How would getting shot help his medical condition?"

Sable stepped toward Bolan, her face earnest and her hands held out in a submissive display. Bolan didn't move. If she had wanted to attack him, her best time would have been while he was dealing with Sanders. She appeared, for her own reasons, to truly want defection to the United States. But he trusted the woman as much as he would a jungle viper.

"Please, let me call him. No harm will come to you if I vouch for you. I have thirty-five thousand euros under a loose panel in the Land Rover. My contact has access to physicians. We can help your friend."

"Stay here," Bolan ordered.

He moved away from the woman without answering her plea. The last thing he wanted was to trust her. He looked at his old friend as he walked toward the blast area. The pilot looked bad, his wounds were grave and he needed medical attention. On his own, Bolan knew he could escape to safety. Taking Sable, his chances shrank drastically. Lugging a wounded friend, those chances became nonexistent.

He quickly surveyed the scene and found no trace of the men who'd been near the helicopter when the missile had landed. He moved past the crater and spotted three corpses still relatively intact. He picked up an AKS-74U that appeared, somewhat miraculously, none too worse for the wear.

Bolan looked up. The fence at the back of the dacha had been blown down. Sanders was crossing the lawn and walked up the right side of the smoking house toward the garage. The agent had been right; if Kubrick had left a security detail with the cars then Sanders was in very real danger.

Bolan spotted a Soviet RPK machine gun, broken like a matchstick. He walked over to the ruined weapon and looked around. Just down the hill from the weapon he saw the corpse of a big man.

He took in the charred business suit stretched over a 250 pound frame. There were the melted remnants of a sling and bandages on the corpse. The face was completely destroyed. He reached over and picked up a beefy fingered hand covered in coarse black hair. He saw the heavy gold signet ring Kubrick had been wearing earlier.

Bolan pulled the ring free and put it in his pocket. DNA analysis could confirm it was Kubrick's.

Bolan stood and attempted to make contact using his sat phone.

"Striker to Aviary."

The same gruff voice answered. "Go ahead, Striker."

"AO sanitized."

"That's good, copy." The voice paused. "Striker we had a frag-op from Mountain Peak."

"Go ahead."

"A mutual friend has been in contact with Mountain Peak."

Bolan nodded. Hal Brognola.

As Bolan approached he saw Sable kneeling beside Jack Grimaldi, adjusting bandages around his wounds. She looked up sharply, raising her pistol. She relaxed when she recognized Bolan, set the pistol beside her and finished tying off Grimaldi's bandages.

"Kubrick?" She asked.

"Dead," Bolan answered. "How is he?"

"Your friend's lost a lot of blood. I don't think a lung was nicked, but I'm afraid of infection. He's starting to feel feverish. We have to get the bullets out."

Bolan knelt beside her and looked down at his old friend. How many times had the Stony Man pilot been there to pull him out of the fire? How many times had Grimaldi served as back up in some violent backwater during Bolan's War Everlasting? He had to do everything he could to save him. Take any chance.

"Your friend *will* die, without immediate help. Have you thought about my offer?" Sable asked.

"There's been a change in the plan." Bolan replied.

It was a rough journey down the mountain, and despite Bolan's best efforts Grimaldi's wounds opened again. His friend was burning with fever and by the time Bolan lowered him to the ground next to Vesler's red Porsche, his breathing was rapid and shallow.

Sanders had already arrived with the Land Rover. As soon as Bolan and Sable appeared, he rushed from hiding to check the Russian agent. He sported two huge black eyes like a bandit mask and his nose was an ugly lump of swollen, purple flesh.

Bolan shrugged out of his jacket and draped it over the wounded pilot. He used a rock to elevate the wounded man's feet. Sable knelt beside Grimaldi again to arrange his bandages after the scramble down to the road. Bolan rose and walked over to the trunk of the Porsche.

He slapped the trunk twice with an open hand. Immediately there was a chorus of muffled shouts and the suspension on the Porsche began to shake.

"Vesler seems fine," Bolan noted.

The sound of sirens could be heard from the valley. Bolan looked at Sable.

"Right, we have to get on the road," he said.

Sanders and Bolan put the unconscious Grimaldi in the back of the Land Rover on top of the folded seats. The pilot's life was in his hands and now depended upon Bolan playing every move exactly right.

"You drive," Bolan told Sable. "Get us down on the highway, extraction is waiting."

"That's what you said last time," she said.

22

Sable started the automobile as Sanders climbed into the back to help support Grimaldi. Bolan stopped, the AKS-74U in his hands. He cocked his head into the wind, squinted in concentration. The sound came to him faintly. With the cacophony of approaching sirens it was hard to pick out, a single whisper in a milling crowd.

"Let's go!" a nervous Sanders called from the back of the Land Rover.

Bolan frowned, ignoring the frightened man. He could almost pick it out. Then the sound solidified enough for him to identify its origins. Bolan moved fast.

The approaching aircraft was coming up the mountain. Bolan sprinted to the Land Rover, jerking open the passenger door. He slid into the passenger seat and slammed the door shut behind him.

"Go!" he shouted.

Sable didn't hesitate. She slammed her foot on the accelerator, and the Land Rover sprayed gravel as it tore out onto the mountain road. The front tires of the all-terrain vehicle hit the pavement and the traction bit hard, increasing the vehicle's speed.

The helicopter flew over the downhill side of the

road and pinned the vehicle in its spotlight. Bolan tried to determine the threat he faced.

The OH-6A Cayuse light observation helicopter spun in front of the Land Rover as the vehicle careened down the winding mountain road.

Bolan half crawled out the open passenger window to bring his weapon into play just as the road dropped sharply around a tight corner. The tires screamed in protest as Sable took the corner too tight for the boxy vehicle's suspension.

The helicopter dropped sharply to keep the racing Land Rover in a tight overwatch position. In that moment, as the chopper banked, Bolan got a clear picture of his pursuer.

Lich had arrived.

The helicopter's doors had been removed and Lich leaned half out of his passenger seat with one foot propped on the landing skid. He had attached a RPK to the top of the helicopter door with a bungee cord. He manipulated the weapon with one hand while bracing himself with the other. Behind him, as anonymous as a storm trooper in his flight suit and helmet, the pilot handled the little helicopter with cool skill.

"Get the floodlight!" Sable screamed as she swerved the Land Rover around another corner. "It's blinding me!"

Bolan thrust the top half of his body out the passenger window and aimed at the bobbing helicopter. His blast went wild, and Lich triggered a burst in response that failed to connect.

The helicopter suddenly shot straight up for a moment and let the racing Land Rover pass below it. Bolan saw the flashing light of the approaching emergency response vehicles. He slid back into the Land Rover's cab and put the assault rifle out of sight under the dash.

Sable blew past the two fire trucks and ambulance doing twice their speed, her foot never straying from the accelerator. Her window was down and her raven hair flew like a tattered banner behind her. Her knuckles were white on the steering wheel as she drove the vehicle expertly, but her face was a serene mask.

Minutes later they took a corner too wide and almost crashed head-on with a police vehicle. Both cars swerved and knocked off their driver's side view mirrors in a metal on metal clap.

Sable screamed curses in Russian but refused to slow. Bolan jerked his head around to stare out the back of the Land Rover, trying to determine how the police car was going to respond to the near miss. He saw brake lights flash red. The police vehicle spun around, starting pursuit.

The Executioner didn't hesitate. He grabbed hold of the handle on the car roof and sat up on the edge of the door through the open window.

As he brought up the rifle, Bolan felt the firm grip of Sable's hand as she grasped the inside of his knee to help steady him. Bolan snapped open the folding stock and shouldered the weapon. Behind the police car Bolan saw Lich's helicopter swinging wide over the valley and bearing down on them.

Bolan looked down the open battlefield sights and triggered a long, ragged burst toward the front of the chasing police vehicle. His rounds skipped off the pavement striking sparks. Tracers poured from the muzzle of his chattering weapon. Smoking shell casings bounced off the roof of the Land Rover and spun out into the night.

The first of Bolan's 5.45 mm slugs tore into the front

grille of the police cruiser and bored into the engine block. The vehicle's hood snapped open and popped straight up as the lock mechanism burst apart. The stream of rushing air grabbed the front hood and flipped it back into the car's windshield.

The driver locked the brakes of his vehicle and went into a sloppy power slide. More rounds struck the front of the vehicle and clawed the engine into scrap metal. The helicopter zoomed in over the stalled police vehicle and charged down on the fleeing Land Rover. The single Cyclops eye of the forward-mounted spotlight blazed out, blinding Bolan.

Tracer rounds began spitting out toward Bolan. Sable locked the brakes hard and took yet another corner in the endless succession of turns, momentarily blocking the helicopter from sight.

Bolan anticipated the helicopter's flight path and shifted so that his weapon was pointed straight across the roof of the Land Rover. Inside the car Sable's hand was still a reassuring anchor on Bolan's leg. Grudgingly, he acknowledged to himself that the woman's driving was phenomenal.

Forced to take the turn in the road wide, just as Bolan had expected, the helicopter swung into view again. Lich and Bolan triggered simultaneous blasts. Bolan, with a sniper's skill, blew out the floodlight on the helicopter undercarriage. Lich's blast raked the side of the Land Rover from front to back just above the wheel wells.

The civilian vehicle was jostled by the impact from the high-caliber slugs, but Sable kept the Land Rover steady. Bolan realized the freelance operative had to have had her vehicle outfitted with at least some armor upgrade in order for the rounds not to have penetrated into the passenger areas of the vehicle.

Despite that, Bolan knew the Land Rover could not long take such damage unanswered. Sooner, rather than later, the vehicle would falter under the assault. Bolan sighted on Lich. Bullets traveled in an arc but fell below the circling helicopter. He twisted again and fired another burst, throwing his rounds wide as Sable powered through yet another turn. The landscape they raced past was a blur to Bolan, and his face and arms were numb from the cold air buffeting him.

Lich had the RPK wide open, making no attempt to control his bursts. Rounds fell around the swerving Land Rover in a deadly hail of lead. Two stray rounds struck the hood of the Land Rover and punched through. One skipped off the radiator and white plumes of steam began spilling out.

Bolan traced a line of 5.45 mm slugs off the Cayuse's passenger-side skid and across the belly of the aircraft. The chopper's undercarriage was perforated by half a dozen bullets, but the helicopter seemed to easily soak up the damage as it leapfrogged over the Land Rover. Bolan twisted, following the helicopter with his weapon blazing. His weapon went empty, and he punched the magazine release button and slid back into the SUV.

"We're almost off the mountain," Sable said.

Now that Bolan was back inside she steered with both hands on the wheel. Bolan felt a detached, floating sensation as the tires of the Land Rover lost grip on the pavement as Sable cornered too sharply. She managed to keep the vehicle from flipping, however.

"Give me a magazine!" Bolan shouted into the back seat.

"From where?" Sanders screamed back.

"Just give me your weapon before they swing back," Bolan snarled.

Laying half sprawled over the still comatose Grimaldi, Sanders watched as Bolan unslung the Bizon-19 Sable had given him from around his chest. He reached into a side pocket and pulled out a spare magazine. Bolan used his thumb to drop the Bizon's empty mag and then injected the fresh clip into the magazine well.

Bolan looked at the submachine gun in disgust. It was a pitiful defense against even such a light helicopter, and it was no match whatsoever for Lich's RPK machine gun. The capability of Lich to stand off beyond the 9 mm weapon's range and return fire with his heavier caliber was obvious. The only modicum of hope Bolan held out was that Lich would need to draw closer to compensate for Sable's erratic driving.

"You think that's going to do any good?" Sable asked.

"I'm thinking I might just try when they get closer."

"Well, you're going to get your chance," Sanders said, thrusting his head up between the seats. "Here they come!"

The Land Rover was out of the twisting decline of the mountain road and entered the valley straight away. The Cayuse spun, put its nose down and came flying directly toward them.

"What does he want?" Sanders screamed in frustration. "He knows he's done!"

"He wants to make sure no good deed goes unpunished," Sable replied.

Bolan thrust the Bizon-19 out the passenger window and opened fire. The Cayuse swooped toward them like a metallic bird of prey. Sable swerved the Land Rover like a drunk as she handled the racing vehicle, but she was trapped within the confines of the road. Nothing but dark the forest, thick with trees, waited on either side of the road.

The helicopter pilot's hand was cold and steady as he guided the bird straight down on them. Lich was merciless. He hung half out of the helicopter pod, foot on the skid, and fired the RPK in a long burst.

Bolan aimed his weapon straight at the glass bubble front of the speeding helicopter. He triggered the submachine gun and fought to keep the jumping, twisting chatter gun on target. Bullets from the RPK ate up fist-sized chunks of the road.

Sable jerked the Land Rover from one side and then snapped it back to the other. She was screaming an unending stream of Russian curses as she drove. In the back, Sanders just screamed.

More bullets ripped through the engine hood of the Land Rover. They clawed their way up and blew out the windshield. Propelled by the wind shear of Sable's speed, glass blew into the cab, forcing Bolan to throw up his arm as a shield.

The Cayuse roared by overhead. Bolan twisted as it passed, still stubbornly returning fire.

Sable shrieked as a 7.62 mm round hit her leg. The new wound was barely an inch below the prior one, and blood spouted hot and sticky across Bolan. The emergency brake set between the passenger's and driver's seat exploded, sending fragments of the hand brake into Bolan's thigh and side.

Hanging outside the window, Bolan kept the Bizon roaring. He poured 9 mm rounds into the low flying helicopter as it passed directly overhead. He saw sparks fly as rounds struck metal, and he noted with grim satisfaction when glass shattered under the impact of the soft-nosed slugs. Bolan grunted in pain at the sudden force of bullet fragments striking his leg. He emptied his magazine as the Cayuse swung out and around.

As he slid back into the Land Rover, The Executioner realized a burst of Lich's fire had penetrated the passenger areas of the vehicle behind him. He felt his throat constrict in the grim realization of what he would find.

Grimaldi was soaked with blood. Bolan twisted and saw Sanders.

The CIA agent had taken multiple rounds in the torso. Lich's machine gun blast had torn him apart, shredding the muscles and bones of his upper rib cage. The man's eyes stared back at Bolan, wide and sightless. His mouth hung slack in death, and his chest looked like ground hamburger. A small sigh escaped his open mouth as his lungs collapsed and he pitched forward.

Bolan shoved the dead man to the side and thrust his fingers onto the side of Grimaldi's neck. He sagged with relief as his fingertips found a pulse, weak and fluttering, but still present.

"Come on, Jack, you tough bastard," Bolan whispered.

Blood leaked from a new wound in the pilot's arm, and Bolan pulled the shredded collar of his flight suit to one side to get a better look. The soldier's adrenaline was pumping so hard he almost laughed out loud in relief when he saw the flesh gouged out of Grimaldi's upper arm. The bullet had grazed his friend but not lodged.

Bolan stuck his finger into the bleeding hole to stem the tide.

"They're coming back!" Sable screamed.

"Drive!" Bolan shouted. "Just drive!"

He ducked and looked out the window. He saw the Cayuse pacing them. The helicopter swung into a parallel course with the speeding Land Rover, flying fast at treetop level. Lich was raising the RPK.

As Lich fired, Sable slammed on the brakes. Unprepared for the maneuver, Bolan was thrown forward, arms flying. He struck the top of the cab and bounced down to hit the dash hard with his ribs. The wind was knocked from him and he turned, sliding down into his seat.

Out to the side of them the Cayuse shot past, and Lich's blast missed them by a wide mark. The helicopter began to sweep back toward their position.

Sable threw open her door and turned to Bolan. "We've got to get into the trees!"

"Go!" Bolan shouted.

Without looking back, the woman jumped from the driver's seat of the Land Rover. Bolan opened his door and jumped out of the vehicle. He winced as pain lanced up from the wound in his thigh, but he did not falter.

Limping badly, Sable made her way toward the dark line of trees beside the highway. Beyond the limits of the Land Rover's headlights Bolan heard the change in pitch as the Cayuse came around and began its approach. He heard the RPK open up again.

Bolan jerked open the rear passenger door, reached in and grabbed Sanders's body by the shirt. He pulled the corpse through the open door, dumping him on the ground.

The roar of the rushing helicopter was deafening as it bore down on Bolan. The sound of bullets eating into the asphalt rang in his ears. Bolan grabbed the unconscious Jack Grimaldi and heaved with all his might. The pilot slid into his arms. Bolan tried to pull him farther out, to get a better grip and drag him toward the safety of the roadside. But Grimaldi's body wouldn't budge, caught somehow half in and half out of the vehicle.

Sable suddenly appeared out of the night at Bolan's side, helping him take Grimaldi's weight despite her own wounds.

Bolan heard the Cayuse coming for them. He threw a look over his shoulder and gauged the distance to the dubious safety of the tree line. He looked toward the helicopter and knew they would never make it. He knew Lich could see them, unarmed and helpless, knew the traitor was loving it.

"Just run," Bolan told the dark-haired woman. "There's no point in you dying, just run."

"What? Miss all the fun? Shut up and pull, Cowboy," Sable replied.

Bolan heaved Grimaldi with all his strength, rushing toward the edge of the road as the Cayuse came down on them for a final run. He backpedaled until his heels crunched on the gravel of the roadside and he knew he'd crossed the road. The helicopter was on them.

Bolan twisted and heaved Grimaldi into the ditch at the road's edge. He shoved Sable down with the wounded Grimaldi, then collapsed on top of them both in the ditch, shielding them with his body. Above him, Lich triggered the RPK.

The bullets stopped suddenly, Bolan heard the roar of massive engines. He heard the powerful burp of miniguns going off and felt rotor wash beating down on him like typhoon winds.

Looking up he saw the gigantic hulk of a CH-47F

hovering over the area, rear cargo ramp lowering. Bolan craned his neck but couldn't see Lich's Cayuse. The big cargo helicopter touched down and men in OD green flight suits ran out holding M-4 carbines. Behind them came two men bearing a stretcher and medic bags.

23

Bolan crouched in the darkness with Sable at his side. They watched the little house on the edge of Tirana in the former republic of Yugoslavia. Inside was Arso Branislava, Claus Lich's middleman.

Bolan and Sable moved out gingerly from behind the shed, leapfrogging and covering each other as they approached the quiet house. Bolan caught up with the woman at the back door. Both had their weapons out and held at the ready.

"Branislava is a key operator in the distribution network for Afghanistan heroin," Sable told Bolan. "After a big deal like the one he just pulled off for Lich, he's going to want to celebrate."

"Will he be too incoherent to interrogate?" Bolan asked.

"Should make it easier. If he's too drunk, we'll just use the adrenaline on him."

"Let's do it," Bolan replied.

The Executioner reflected on what he'd learned in the past twenty-four hours. According to Brognola, Jack Grimaldi was in rough shape but was expected to make a full recovery. Claus Lich had disappeared and was believed to have taken the Gustav prototype with him.

Sable had informed Bolan that the prototype was the technological lynchpin in the equipment used to enrich uranium into nuclear material.

ARSO BRANISLAVA WAS JARRED from his stupor to find his well-paid bodyguards were bloody corpses. Working together, Bolan and Sable had little trouble making the mercenary-fixer talk. There was absolutely zero percentage in dying for Lich, prized client or not.

"Claus is gone!" Branislava cried. "The Gustav prototype is in the city, it is here," he sputtered. "But Lich left last night. For Argentina."

24

The Executioner got out of the car.

He left it running, and the low powerful rumbling of its engine was the only noise he heard. He looked up and down the residential street set among the bluffs overlooking the city proper. It was quiet. No dogs barked, no cars drove on the street.

Bolan pulled on a pair of snug, dark gloves.

He walked around to the back of his car and opened the trunk. The Kevlar vest Bolan wore under his leather jacket accented his size. He wore a black knit watch cap pulled down low.

Reaching into the trunk, he removed the false bottom where the tire jack was kept and pulled out a cut-down assault rifle. It was stubby with a shortened front grip and compact muzzle. A sound suppressor had been screwed into the modified barrel.

Bolan looked around. Again, he saw no one and he held the carbine down by his side. He closed his trunk and pulled a cell phone from the pocket of his jacket. He keyed the walkie-talkie mode and spoke a brief word into the microphone.

"Arlington."

There was a pause. It went on for too long.

"Arlington," he repeated.

"Sable," came the reply.

Bolan changed functions on his phone. He hit a number on his speed dial and put the phone back in his pocket before the connection was made. He started up the sidewalk toward the house.

The cell phone signal connected. Its twin, a half-mile away, rang once. The explosion at the utility substation was small, about equal in sound to that of an automobile backfiring. Bolan didn't believe in being gratuitous.

The transformer governing power grid for the street below. Streetlights cut out. Porch lights and the blue glow of televisions seen through windows went dark as well. As did night lights, clocks, computers and home alarm systems.

Bolan snapped the bolt back on the receiver of his carbine and let it slide forward, locking and loading the weapon. Reaching up, he pulled the balaclava hood over his face.

The soldier broke into an easy, loping jog. Speed, surprise and aggression were the foundational points of the operation. He turned up the driveway and headed down the east side of the house. He noted the red SUV he'd been told about. Beside it was a white Volvo he hadn't been informed of. He held the assault rifle up by its pistol grip and reached out with one hand as he came up to the low gate set in the concrete block wall fencing in the backyard.

The Executioner cleared the wall in an easy hop, landed in a crouch on the other side and brought the muzzle of his weapon up immediately. He scanned the area, looking for signs of movement from the house or in the yard itself. He counted down to the third window he'd been told was the master bedroom.

He sidled up next to the window and pulled out his clip knife. He used the thumb post to slide the well oiled blade open with one hand.

Moving carefully, Bolan inserted the tip of the knife under the lip of the window screen. With an easy motion he popped out the screen. His eyes never left the master bedroom window.

The Executioner rose from his crouch and took the assault rifle in both hands.

Then all hell broke loose.

EMIL AIRAPETIAN PUT his head down and pressed his right nostril shut. With his other hand he took a customized gold straw and moved it into the opposite nostril. He lowered his head and sniffed long and hard, running his face down the short, thick line of cocaine he'd spread out on the etched glass of the mirror. Coming to the end of the white powder, The man snorted the last of it, then threw his head back as if trying to stop a nose bleed.

He sagged into the support of his seat as blood rushed to his brain. Clear mucus ran from his nostril immediately, and with his head tilted back it carried the coke out of his sinus cavity and trickled it down his throat, numbing it pleasantly. Euphoria hit him a heartbeat later and he opened his eyes wide.

Airapetian let his head roll back against the top of the chair in his master bedroom. Suddenly everything plunged into darkness.

Airapetian was a narcoterrorist and weapons trafficker by trade. He'd stopped believing in coincidences a long time ago in the streets of Tirana's poorest neighborhoods. When he realized his electricity had gone out, his fear was immediate.

Springing forward, he yanked open the drawer of his nightstand and pulled out his pistol. The Ruger P-95 loaded with a round chambered and the safety off.

He caught a flash of movement from the corner of his eye and saw the screen to his window pulled away.

Outside a shadow moved and Airapetian started firing.

ABOVE BOLAN A SUDDEN FUSILLADE of pistol shots exploded and bullets punched out through the master bedroom window, shattering glass into glittering shrapnel. Operating on pure reflex, Bolan spun around and dropped to one knee. He held the assault rifle sideways above his head and sprayed the interior of the room with one long, ragged burst.

Bolan poured the 5.56 mm rounds into the room, using the spray to suppress the pistol marksman. He had to assume it was his primary target. Arso Branislava had specified no bodyguards, only a near certain likelihood that Airapetian was heavily armed. Bolan cut of his burst after about twelve rounds and stood, flipping around so his back was pressed to the wall beside the window.

No return fire came through the window. With the element of surprise gone it would be suicide to backlight his silhouette. Bolan knew time was running out. His ears still rang from the gunshots that had rendered his sound suppressor laughably useless.

He had to assume the police were on their way. Bolan knew what would happen to him if he was caught by the Serbian police. He'd disappear into a Belgrade prison and that would be the end of him.

Even as those thoughts raced through his mind, Bolan gave no consideration to running.

Swinging the weapon around, Bolan thrust the muzzle through the broken window, eyes tracking for the slightest sense of movement. He saw none. His eyes took in the scene.

His suppressive fire had torn ragged holes in the wall across from the window. The bed had been ripped apart and pillows shredded. A heavy nightstand lay blown apart in one corner.

Shots rang out from the corner of the room where Bolan spotted the doorway. He saw movement as muzzle-flashes lit up the darkness.

The automatic carbine jumped in his hands and the bolt receiver snapped back and forth faster than the eye could follow, spilling spent cartridges onto the floor. Bolan's night vision was ruined by the muzzle-flashes, and he could only make out impressions inside the heavily shadowed room.

Bolan stopped firing.

He saw the door to the bedroom standing wide open and caught a glimpse of hallway past it. Another door, presumably to the master bathroom, stood ajar. In the distance Bolan heard the wailing of sirens.

The target was a wanted man, and he had no more to gain from police contact than Bolan. That meant now that his cover was blown, he'd be making for the front door and his vehicle rather than chance getting caught in a police barricade. Bolan turned back from the window, his decision made.

The Executioner freed his cell phone while he ran and punched the function back to walkie-talkie. Coming up to the gate, he didn't vault it this time. He quickly scanned the area before opening the gate from the inside.

Holding his weapon one-handed, he said, "Primary active. Provide cover."

"Affirmative." Sable's voice was a cool salve to Bolan in his hyperalert state.

He put the phone away and moved forward in a sideways scuttle that covered ground but left him centered and on balance to get a shot off if he needed to react to gunfire. He looked out into the street. He saw faces in the dark windows across the road but didn't see any bystanders out on the pavement yet.

These people had lived through a brutal suppression of the Kosovo Liberation Army by Serbian commandos and special police units. People knew to keep their heads down when the guns started firing in the middle of the night.

Coming to the side of the house, Bolan prepared himself.

A figure ran out the front door with a pistol stuck in the front of his pants and a rifle in one hand. A small leather suitcase was tightly clutched in the man's other fist. There was a shriek of locking brakes and squealing tires as two patrol cars slid around the corner and sped down the street heading straight for the house.

The man never hesitated as he ran toward his Lexus SUV. He simply lifted the rifle single-handed and triggered a heavy burst into the oncoming police car.

The safety glass cracked and dented as rounds marched up the hood of the car and impacted the windshield. Both black-uniformed officers threw their hands up in futile attempts to ward off the burst of automatic fire. The rounds tore into them and splashed them across the inside of their car.

The speeding vehicle struck another car in a residential driveway. The gunman turned and stitched another burst down the side of the vehicle, gouging pockmarks across the door. The second police car's driver slammed on the brakes and threw the vehicle into reverse. The shooter turned and lifted his rifle across the hood of his red SUV.

His head exploded on the impact of a single 7 mm round fired by Sable. Bolan's own burst caught the narcoterrorist in the small of his back and hacked away big chunks of flesh. Ripped apart by the cross fire, the Armenian sprawled across the hood of his vehicle before sliding off and falling onto the driveway. The black suitcase fell from his limp grip and fell on the street.

Both officers in the second vehicle crawled out of their car on the side facing away from the terrorist gunman. Unaware of third party involvement, they both began rapid-firing their pistols at the side of the Lexus SUV facing them. Its windows shattered and lead bullets rang off metal.

Bolan realized his own car was directly in their line of fire. The scenario had gone to hell in a handbasket faster then anyone could have expected. Bolan knew once he grabbed the suitcase he could never make it to his car across the open field of fire covered by the officers. Already, the city behind the firing policemen sounded like it was alive with sirens, all of them descending on this spot. He was pinned down. Trapped.

Then Sable made his decision for him.

25

Without warning 7 mm rounds punched through the thin skin of the police vehicle. A round entered one door, passed through the cab then penetrated the driver's side door. It struck the crouching Serbian high in the chest and slammed him to the ground.

The Executioner ran for the suitcase. He fired a short burst from his assault rifle to cover his movement, but the act was unnecessary as Sable's rounds had left the lone, outgunned policeman cowering behind what cover he could find.

Bolan went to a knee beside the SUV. He set down his rifle and quickly worked the snaps on the case, popping open the lid. Looking inside he saw a device set into cut foam that matched the schematic drawings Barbara Price had sent to him from Stony Man Farm.

"I have confirmation," Bolan said into his cell phone as he secured the suitcase.

"Copy," Sable answered. "Get out of there."

Bolan grabbed the case and ran for it.

Reaching his vehicle, he threw open the door and tossed the suitcase into the passenger's seat. He dropped his nearly spent magazine and reached around behind his back and pulled another one from his belt. The assault rifle locked in the bolt open position and it snapped home as he seated the new magazine. In rapid succession five new patrol cars roared into the street. Sable took out the driver of the first vehicle and the car rushed forward, driverless, to smash into the initial patrol car.

Bolan slid behind the wheel and slammed the car into reverse. The Audi was an automatic, which wasn't as good for precision driving, but it was what had been available. The flip side of this was that it would be easier for Bolan to fire on the move than in a standard transmission.

Bolan hit the gas and the car shot backward, building speed.

He gunned the car back up the residential street, away from the police units. He'd been sent an aerial photo of the neighborhood and had taken time to memorize a street map of the area. He had a plan and he was committed to following it down to the last ticking second.

Coming to the end of the street, Bolan jumped the curb and tore across a brief stretch of private lawn.

The vehicle plunged down a short hill and over several low, decorative bushes before popping out onto a parallel street. A car blared its horn and swerved to avoid Bolan as he yanked the emergency brake and slid the Audi through a precision bootlegger maneuver. Facing the proper direction, Bolan pushed the accelerator down and the car surged forward.

He set the smoking assault rifle on the seat next to him and flipped open his cell phone. He passed more police cars racing in the other direction.

"Arlington clear."

There was no response.

Throwing the phone down, Bolan looked in his rearview mirror but saw none of the siren carriers slam into a skid and wheel their vehicles around. He jerked the car to the right and down a side street heading for his rally point with Sable.

Four blocks later Bolan shot underneath an overpass and quickly guided the car off the road, sliding to a stop. With tight, efficient motions he transferred the Gustav implement out of the suitcase and into one Barbara Price had provided for him.

That done he pulled back into the street and sped another mile through twisting streets toward the edge of the city. Within minutes Bolan had pulled up to the rally point. The woman appeared out of the shadows of an abandoned gas station almost immediately.

Her weapon already broken down and inside a carrying case, Sable climbed into the seat next to Bolan.

"You get the Gustav?" she asked.

"It's in the back seat."

"Good," Sable answered. "Then I can give you what my contact gave me before we took Airapetian down."

"What?" Bolan asked sharply.

She held up a Montblanc pen. Quickly she unscrewed the writing instrument and showed Bolan the tightly rolled microfiche strip inside. Once Bolan had acknowledged seeing what she'd showed him, Sable put the pen back together again and slipped it into a pocket.

"Three months ago I used Sanders to install a sleeper code into Lich's expense account activities. We were able to trace him siphoning off operational funds into black accounts, then from the black accounts into dummy corporation personal accounts. One of the accounts was flagged as being active yesterday—for an amount identical to what Airapetian paid for the Gustav implement."

Sable lifted her pistol and pressed the muzzle against Bolan's head.

Bolan stiffened behind the wheel of the speeding automobile. The Russian agent slid her free hand across the broad expanse of Bolan's hard chest and freed his Beretta from its shoulder holster. Without looking she powered down the car's automatic window and tossed the gun out.

"What are you doing?" Bolan asked, keeping his voice flat.

"Pull over. My fire selector is on 3-round burst. You don't have a prayer," the woman said.

Bolan kept driving. He pressed his foot down on the accelerator. The odometer began to creep up.

"Ballsy." Sable's voice was cold. "But I'll take the gamble. I have an air bag. You have a pistol against your temple."

"I saved your life."

"I won't kill you unless I have to."

"I should believe you?"

"About this? Yes. If I were lying, I would have opened up as soon as I got into the car."

"All of this was just a ploy to get the Gustav once Lich beat you to it?" Bolan asked.

"I was depending on Sanders. You realize, of course, who originally helped in the design of the new generation Gustav, don't you?"

"Claus Lich." Bolan shook his head. "Have you always been an evil bitch?"

"I'm hurt," Sable mocked. "I'm a free market capitalist. Now slow down and pull over, damn it, or I will kill you."

"You'll kill me anyway," Bolan said. "You know I'll come after you."

"If not you then someone else," Sable rationalized. "Where I'm going I won't be followed."

"Which is?"

"Nice try."

"You can't stay hidden forever."

"Tell that to Osama bin Laden," Sable said with a laugh.

"That's some life."

"He doesn't have my connections."

The Executioner seemed to struggle with some inner decision. His foot eased up on the accelerator. She had the drop on him. He thought about disarming her, but he'd seen her in action. He could take her, but not like this. He pulled over to the side of the road.

They were in an a rural residential area where small family plots of land were interspersed with orchards. The road was lonely this time of night. Up ahead, on a tiny, single lane runway, a pilot was waiting for them.

Bolan sighed and put his hands on top of the Audi's steering wheel. He would have turned to look at Sable, but the muzzle of her pistol was still flush with his temple.

"Don't do this," he said.

"It's already done."

"In the wrong hands that device is a death warrant for millions."

"You're assuming that I believe your hands are safe hands."

"What about your deal with the U.S. government? If it wasn't enough money, then why didn't you just ask for more?" Bolan tried to stall.

"Get out of the car," The Russian agent ordered.

Bolan reached over and grabbed the handle to the car

door. He pulled on it and let the door open an inch. The dome light over their heads came on, illuminating them in a halo of light. Sable's hand was rock steady as she held the muzzle of her pistol against Bolan's head.

"You saved my life at the dacha," Sable said. "Don't make me kill you now."

Bolan pushed the car door open the rest of the way. He put one foot out of the car onto the ground. The gravel on the side of the road crunched under his foot. He shifted his weight on that leg and leaned toward the open door.

"One thing," Sable suddenly said.

"What?"

Bolan paused, his muscles tensed to push him up off the seat and out the open door.

"Speaking of the dacha, I still owe you for something."

Sable swung her free hand from behind her back. Bolan caught the motion and instinctively pulled away, but his center of balance was awkward and he never had a chance to defend himself.

Sable's Taser swung into Bolan. He spasmed hard under the electrical juice. He felt every muscle in his body violently seize up as blinding pain lanced through his body. He made a hard gurgling sound and bit down on his tongue hard enough to draw blood.

Suddenly the intense pain vanished. Bolan sagged forward, completely limp as his muscles unknotted. He hit the steering wheel of the car and began to slide off it.

Sable hit him again.

Bolan arched upward, thrusting his chest out. His limbs clenched tight on his frame again. His neck became a rigid column of muscle and his bloody teeth were bared in a fierce, involuntary grimace. His vision went white for an instant, and he could no longer see or hear. He jerked under the voltage and slammed his head against the roof of the car.

Suddenly the pain was gone again.

Bolan sank into the seat, collapsing. Sable lifted the butt of her pistol and slammed it into the side of Bolan's head, knocking him over. His head pitched out of the car and he fell half out of the driver's seat.

Sable shifted and twisted in her seat. She lifted her foot, curling her leg up tight against her body. She kicked out hard, striking Bolan with the heel of her boot into his upper ribs.

The blow shoved Bolan clear of the car and he flopped out of the vehicle and hit the ground. Blood dripped from his mouth and his vision swam. He heard Sable say something from behind him in a voice he was sure was mocking—but he couldn't make out the words.

Then his ears popped, and in a rush of sound Bolan found he could hear again. He heard the idle of the car engine, smelled the exhaust pouring out of the tailpipe so close to his head. He tasted the metallic tang of blood in his mouth.

"Consider this a gift, then," Sable finished.

Bolan felt a slender object strike his back between his shoulder blades. He knew instinctively that it was the pen Sable had showed him earlier. The one with the trail of money leading to Lich's door. She was tossing Bolan a bone. He knew it wasn't a favor. She was arranging to have him do her dirty work for her.

He tried to push himself up, but he was still too weak from the electrocution. He felt a line of bloody drool roll out of his mouth.

"It was never personal," Sable said.

He heard the door to the vehicle slam shut behind him. Sable floored it and the tires spun, spraying Bolan with gravel.

He fell forward and rested his spinning head in his arms. The vehicle fishtailed out onto the road and sped off. Bolan lifted his head and saw the red taillights as the triple agent raced away.

The briefcase, designed to last-minute specifications under Barbara Price's supervision by Cowboy Kissenger and containing the Gustav implement, was in the back seat of the Audi. That implement was just as dangerous as unsupervised nuclear warheads when traded on the open market.

Bolan rolled over. He knew he was lucky to be alive.

He pulled out his cell phone and followed the instructions Price had given him.

"It's not you," Bolan said out loud. "I can't let that Gustav go."

Bolan keyed up the speed-dial function on his phone. Then he hit a button and sent the signal out over the network. There was a momentary pause while the signal bounced off an orbital satellite and connected to the passive receiver buried in the frame of the briefcase carrying the Gustav implement.

In the car, Bolan knew Sable would hear the first ring as the connection was made.

Down the road the explosion came sharp and loud and the gas going up tripped hard on the heels of the initial explosion. A ball of fire shot into the air and turned the night as bright as day for a brief, blinding flash.

Out from the fireball the twisted, burned pieces of the Audi began to fall in chunks and ash. Barely two hundred yards away, Bolan felt the vibrating concussion of the blast and a wave of heat rolled over him.

The remains of the car sat in the middle of the road and blazed as gas and engine fluids continued to burn in a smear across the asphalt. Bolan gritted his teeth and forced himself up onto his feet.

He looked up the stretch of road toward the funeral pyre that consumed the Russian operative.

"It was never personal," Bolan said.

26

Claus Lich's villa sat on Barracas Street in Buenos Aires, Argentina.

Buenos Aires was a city unlike any other in Latin America. To most tourists it seemed like a first world, industrial European city placed on the wrong continent. Despite the poverty infamous in the hemisphere, Buenos Aires was rich in appearance and sparkling clean.

But Mack Bolan was no tourist and he wasn't there to admire the scenery.

Since the economic crisis at the turn of the new century, it was possible get an entrée, appetizer and a bottle of wine for the equivalent of three dollars or less—as long as the customer was paying with U.S. dollars instead of the drastically reduced in value peso.

Claus Lich had taken advantage of such currency devaluation to purchase an entire building for his retirement residence. The structure was a refurbished historical building he remodeled and turned into upscale, luxury living quarters. The street, featuring art and French-style buildings, was considered the equivalent of Soho in Manhattan. In addition to wealth, Lich had secured a chic lifestyle with his treason.

Bolan picked out his infiltration route carefully.

Around him the city was subdued by the lateness of the hour. He moved quickly toward his jump point.

The soldier approached the retaining wall set between the commercial parking structure annex and Lich's residence. He scanned the area. Ensuring that he was unobserved he leaped to grasp the outer edge of the high wall. His shimmy technique was precise fieldcraft taught to urban assault climbers in the special operations community.

The strain on his body was prodigious. His wrists ached and the muscles of his arms and shoulders clenched tightly. Displaying great strength, Bolan inched his way up the wall. Once secure, he pulled himself over the edge and scrambled onto the narrow summit. From there he quickly centered his gravity and rose into a crouch.

Bolan shuffled forward, moving across the narrow space until he reached the anchor point where the retaining wall connected with Lich's building. Bolan stretched to the limits of his height and slid his fingers into a shallow bevel line traversing a ornate facade on the building's rear wall.

Three stories up, he swung out into space, carrying the weight of his body and kit onto the strength of his grip. He slowly inched his way along the bevel line. The muscles across his back bunched like straining animals under his clothes, and his brow furrowed with the intensity of his concentration.

Five yards away Bolan reached an ornate windowsill. He stretched out and wrapped his already straining fingers around the lip. It was flat and smooth, offering him no purchase. The only thing that would hold him from the inevitable fall would be the downward force he was able to concentrate through his fingertips in counterbalance to the weight of his body.

Keeping his momentum to a tight minimum, Bolan eased himself out underneath the windowsill. He moved his other hand quickly into position and pulled himself up so he could rest his elbows on the windowsill. The window was open to a three-inch gap to let night breeze enter.

Bolan reached out with an underhand grip and slid his fingers around the bottom of the open window. He pulled himself up until he rested his knees on the window ledge. Once there he rotated around until his buttocks rested on the edge. He shoved the window open.

As soon as there was enough space, Bolan swung his legs through the opening and slid inside the building. He landed in a crouch and quickly slid over to the side to avoid silhouetting himself against the window. He paused for a moment, holding his breath.

He was in.

INSIDE THE VILLA Bolan slid his night-vision goggles into place. Behind him the circuit box for the building hung open and vandalized, cloaking the rooms in darkness. Bolan began his careful infiltration.

Moving silently, he navigated staircases and doorways. He glided through dark rooms like a specter of death. He was a night fighter in his element, and the cold hand of justice was coming for the worst kind of sinner—the betrayer of trusts, the traitor.

Bolan rose like a shadow from the darkness.

The bodyguard heard a noise and turned too late. Bolan fell on him like predator on prey. He smashed a hard forearm into the side of the man's head, knocking him out cold.

Bolan stepped over the man and pushed his way deeper into Claus Lich's residence.

CLAUS LICH'S HOME was a suite of remodeled rooms on the top floor of the building. The Executioner moved through the connecting rooms like a tiger stalking its prey. He moved carefully, weapon out, his night-vision goggles illuminating his path deeper into the villa's uppermost level.

He heard a door open somewhere inside the suite of rooms. He hurried up to a door and pressed his back to one side of it, pistol raised by the side of his head.

From the next room Bolan heard Lich's voice croaking instructions in Spanish. A female voice murmured a reply Bolan didn't catch. Lich's voice was slurred and thick, and Bolan guessed the man was on heavy painkillers following facial reconstructive surgery.

The door beside Bolan swung inward. Bolan tensed. A beam of white light preceded the figure into the room, playing along the carpet as the person walked forward. Bolan extended his sound-suppressed Beretta. The pistol was steady in his fist.

A nurse walked into the room. Bolan easily made out the curves of her body. Inside the goggle faceplate Bolan squeezed one eye shut to prevent a loss of night vision as the illumination from the flashlight beam stretched the dampeners on the NVGs to their limit for a brief moment.

The nurse halted.

The muzzle of the sound suppressor was less than six inches from the back of the woman's head. Bolan's finger tensed on the trigger. He slowly eased up any play. The weapon was poised, ready to fire. The nurse played her flashlight around the antechamber, her head twisting left and right as she looked for something.

"Eduardo?" she asked.

Bolan waited.

The nurse exhaled a heavy sigh and then strode forward purposefully. Crossing the room, she opened the door Bolan had just entered and walked out, pulling it closed behind her.

Bolan moved into the dark bedroom. Silently he approached the massive bed where Lich lay. A line of clear tubing ran from a fluids bag on an IV stand down to the crook of Lich's exposed arm. The man's face was covered in bandages, and his bedside table held a pitcher of water and several prescription bottles.

"Gloria?" Lich asked, voice fuzzy.

Bolan stepped closer to the bed and looked down at the man. Lich's bandaged head turned in his direction. Lich raised his hand in a sudden move, as if he'd been expecting Bolan.

Once again, the Executioner had anticipated Lich's response.

The Beretta 93-R spit flame.

NEUTRON FORCE

The ultimate stealth weapon is in the hands
of an unknown enemy...

A grim presidential directive comes down to
Stony Man: an unknown entity is in possession of
one of the deadliest weapons known to man, and the
death toll across the globe is mounting. It's a silent
murdering machine, killing with no heat, no noise,
no radiation—just silent, invisible slaughter from
ultrafast, subatomic particles. With no nation able
to defend against it, Stony Man's only option is to
destroy it. But first, they must find it....

*Available
June 2007
wherever
you buy books.*

Or order your copy now by sending your name, address, zip or postal code, along with a check or money order (please do not send cash) for $6.50 for each book ordered ($7.99 in Canada), plus 75¢ postage and handling ($1.00 in Canada), payable to Gold Eagle Books, to:

In the U.S.
Gold Eagle Books
3010 Walden Avenue
P.O. Box 9077
Buffalo, NY 14269-9077

In Canada
Gold Eagle Books
P.O. Box 636
Fort Erie, Ontario
L2A 5X3

Please specify book title with your order.
Canadian residents add applicable federal and provincial taxes.

GSM89

JAMES AXLER
DEATH LANDS
Sky Raider

Raw determination in a land of horror...and hope

In the tortured but not destroyed lands of apocalyptic madness of Deathlands, few among the most tyrannical barons can rival the ruthlessness of Sandra Tregart. With her restored biplane, she delivers death from the skies to all who defy her supremacy — a virulent ambition that challenges Ryan Cawdor and his band in unfathomable new ways.

Available June 2007 wherever books are sold.

Or order your copy now by sending your name, address, zip or postal code, along with a check or money order (please do not send cash) for $6.50 for each book ordered ($7.99 in Canada), plus 75¢ postage and handling ($1.00 in Canada), payable to Gold Eagle Books, to:

In the U.S.

Gold Eagle Books
3010 Walden Avenue
P.O. Box 9077
Buffalo, NY 14269-9077

In Canada

Gold Eagle Books
P.O. Box 636
Fort Erie, Ontario
L2A 5X3

Please specify book title with your order.
Canadian residents add applicable federal and provincial taxes.

GDL78

TAKE 'EM FREE
2 action-packed novels plus a mystery bonus
NO RISK
NO OBLIGATION TO BUY

SPECIAL LIMITED-TIME OFFER

Mail to: Gold Eagle Reader Service™

IN U.S.A.: P.O. Box 1867, Buffalo, NY 14240-1867
IN CANADA: P.O. Box 609, Fort Erie, Ontario L2A 5X3

YEAH! Rush me 2 FREE Gold Eagle® novels and my FREE mystery bonus. If I don't cancel, I will receive 6 hot-off-the-press novels every other month. Bill me at the low price of just $29.94* for each shipment. That's a savings of over 10% off the combined cover prices and there is NO extra charge for shipping and handling! There is no minimum number of books I must buy. I can always cancel at any time simply by returning a shipment at your cost or by returning any shipping statement marked "cancel." Even if I never buy another book from Gold Eagle, the 2 free books and mystery bonus are mine to keep forever.

166 ADN EF29   366 ADN EF3A

Name	(PLEASE PRINT)	
Address		Apt. No.
City	State/Prov.	Zip/Postal Code

Signature (if under 18, parent or guardian must sign)

Not valid to current Gold Eagle® subscribers.
Want to try two free books from another series? Call 1-800-873-8635.

* Terms and prices subject to change without notice. N.Y. residents add applicable sales tax. Canadian residents will be charged applicable provincial taxes and GST. This offer is limited to one order per household. All orders subject to approval. Credit or debit balances in a customer's account(s) may be offset by any other outstanding balance owed by or to the customer. Please allow 4 to 6 weeks for delivery.

Your Privacy: Worldwide Library is committed to protecting your privacy. Our Privacy Policy is available online at www.eHarlequin.com or upon request from the Reader Service. From time to time we make our lists of customers available to reputable firms who may have a product or service of interest to you. If you would prefer we not share your name and address, please check here. ☐

GE07

JAKE STRAIT
DAY OF JUDGMENT
BY FRANK RICH

INNER-CITY HELL JUST FOUND A NEW SAVIOR— THE BOGEYMAN

The damned, the dirty and the depraved all call the confines of inner-city hell home. And that's exactly where Jake Strait finds himself when a gorgeous blond angel hires him to infiltrate a religious sect to find her sister. But what he discovers instead is a wild-eyed prophet on the make, putting everyone at risk.

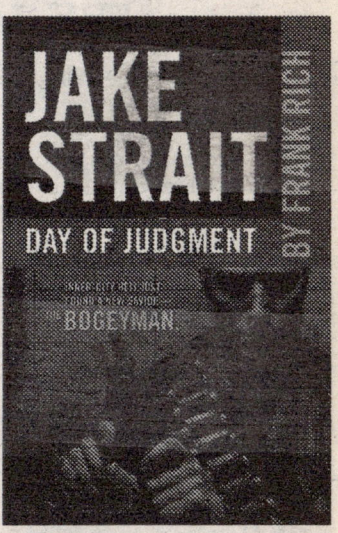

Available July 2007, wherever you buy books.

AleX Archer
THE LOST SCROLLS

In the right hands, ancient knowledge can save a struggling planet...

Ancient scrolls recovered among the charred ruins of the Library of Alexandria reveal astonishing knowledge that could shatter the blueprint of world energy—and archaeologist Annja Creed finds herself an unwilling conspirator in a bid for the control of power.

Available May 2007 wherever you buy books.